I0769210

THE Family Gold

Jerry D Corbin

Third Edition

Originally published 02/10/2020, this third edition includes updated content, editing, and formatting.

ISBN Paperback	979-8-9856587-4-3
ISBN Hardback	979-8-9856587-3-6
ISBN e-Book	979-8-9856587-5-0

Published by Little Joe Publishing
Printed in the United States of America

Copyright 2019 by Jerry D. Corbin

Author's Note

Some stories find you.

I didn't set out to write fiction. I set out to uncover the truth—buried in newspaper clippings, genealogy, and whispered memories.

What I found was gold.

This book was inspired by real people, real history, and a legacy passed down through bloodlines. While much of the story is rooted in my own genealogical research and historical study, I have fictionalized names, events, and places to honor privacy and enhance the narrative.

It's not just a novel. It's a family record wrapped in mystery.

Thank you for walking this journey with me.

Disclaimer

This is a work of fiction. While inspired in part by my passion for history and a detailed study of my family's genealogy, all characters, places, and incidents are either products of my imagination or used fictitiously. Any resemblance to actual persons, living or deceased, or events similar to real occurrences is entirely coincidental. In such instances, I disclaim all responsibility.

— Jerry D. Corbin

Acknowledgements

Thank You, Jesus.

To my wife, Vicky–thank you for believing in me and your unwavering support.

To my father, Clarence William "C.W." Corbin–for the swift kick. You're gone, but you still motivate me.

To my daughters, Summer and Carley–thank you for your constant support and encouragement.

For Research Assistance:

- Victoria Corbin
- Glenn & Better Stroup
- East Tennessee State University
- City of Johnson City, Tennessee
- City of Charleston, South Carolina
- City of Beaver Falls, Pennsylvania

For Additional Help and Support:

- Beaver Valley Writers Guild

Special Thanks To:

- Sparografix – Cover design

To the Best Editor

- Emily Blake
  emilyblakepubcoach@gmail.com

This book is dedicated to my mother,

Macel DeLoach Corbin

Thank you for inspiring me with a rich family history and unforgettable stories that simply had to be told.

Table of Contents

PART I

Robert Bailey

Chapter 1

The Confederate Treasure

My uncle always told me, "There is no escaping our choices or the consequences of those actions. Good or bad, wise or foolish, they're all connected, and we own them all equally and forever. Whenever there is quiet time, they return to please or haunt us—moments of great joy or pain, people you love or those who wish ill of you. Their images hover ominously close, so you dare not open your eyes. The memories always win because we own them. They are a part of us. What calls them to us, I do not know. But when they come, you will not have peace; you must endure because they're yours."

I never understood what he meant. Last night, my sleep was haunted by the ghosts of deeds and memories I thought had long since been laid to rest.

As I contemplated these things, I realized it was my uncle who concerned me. He had not been acting himself lately. Last time I saw him, a piece of paper fell from his pocket as he rode off. By the time I retrieved it, he was gone. On the paper were just four words. I didn't understand their meaning, but they concerned me.

***

My name is Robert Bailey. I am a magistrate in Johnson City, Tennessee. My wife, Mary, and I have lived here all our lives. We work a small tobacco farm in the foothills of the Great Smoky Mountains.

Mary says I was the best catch in town. I don't know about that, but I've learned one thing: no life touched by gold is ever ordinary. Mine is extraordinary!

Johnson City was chartered by the State of Tennessee in 1869 and is located near the base of the Smokies, on the eastern side of the state. We share a history with famous people like Daniel Boone, Andrew Jackson, and General A. E. Jackson, who is buried in the old Jonesborough cemetery.

The soil is bright, reddish-orange clay, and is generally too rocky for farming. A few wide valleys along the foothills have decent soil, but they are scarce.

For that reason, you won't find large vegetable crops grown here. Folks only grow what they need to survive. One crop that does well is Burley tobacco, a light, airy tobacco that needs to air-cure for eight or more weeks. It is the chief money crop in these parts. At harvest time, leaves are hung on wooden rods in the barn and left to cure by the air circulating in and around them. About a quarter of the farmers here earn their living from tobacco.

Folks around these parts aren't wealthy. We work hard for everything we have, but we like it here, and we love those mountains. A hazy blue mist, almost like smoke, usually hides the tops of the mountain ridges—hence the name, "Smoky

Mountains", and there is no more beautiful sight in the whole world.

Our story begins on October 17th, 1898. My Uncle, James Tennessee Adams, spent the evening with Mary and me, as we were to travel together to a wedding the following evening. After Mary retired, we spent the rest of that warm autumn evening sipping one of the finest jugs to be found in Johnson City. Tennessee came up through a hardscrabble life, and every line in his face had a story behind it. He was a tall, handsome man for his age, with deep-set eyes. His hair was always neatly cut and combed. His ruddy, sunbaked skin was mostly covered by whiskers, some sandy blond and others white. He was plain-spoken and fond of the drink. He loved telling stories and grew quite loquacious—while I was a good listener. That night, he told me how he enlisted on September 14[th,] 1863, in the Tennessee Cavalry at Johnson City and served to the end of hostilities in 1865.

***

Abraham Lincoln's Vice President, Andrew Johnson of Greeneville, Tennessee, had been Governor of Tennessee before the war, which helped sway loyalty to the North.

Washington County was divided in its loyalties between pro-Union and pro-secession sentiments.

During a referendum on June 8, 1861, the County voted in favor of staying in the Union. So it was that Uncle Tennessee's Company M, 8th Cavalry, became part of the Union Army.

He had been shot a time or two and captured once, serving several months in Libby Prison in Richmond, Virginia, before being traded for Confederate prisoners.

Libby Prison in Richmond, Virginia

Toward the end of the war, in those desperate days in April of 1865, Richmond found itself under attack by General Grant's army. General Robert E. Lee knew his tattered, unfed army could no longer defend the capital. Richmond was sure to fall, so on Sunday, April 2, 1865, he gave Confederate President Jefferson Davis two days to save what he could and flee the city.

Davis left that evening on a train to Danville, Virginia. Under the supervision of Navy Captain William H. Parker, a second train followed Davis with the War Department Treasury of $300,000 in Union currency and $500,000 in gold and silver: gold ingots, gold double eagle coins, silver coins, silver bricks, and Mexican silver dollars. Captain Parker was charged with putting together a troop to protect not only the South's most important executives but also its treasure. The only personnel available for this task were midshipmen from a training ship on the James River—for the most part, they were fresh Navy personnel in training. Some were only children, as young as twelve.

The two trains left Richmond at midnight. In Danville,

President Davis and his staff were given horses to ride. The treasure was loaded into wagons, and they all headed to the old U.S. Mint in Greensboro, North Carolina.

Uncle Tennessee's Company M was sent to prevent President Davis's escape. Their mission was to overcome the President's forces, capture Davis, and seize the gold.

The Cavalry rode hard and beat Captain William H. Parker to Greensboro, forcing him to change his plans. The treasure was loaded into used sugar, coffee, flour, and ammunition containers; then Parker headed southwest. They traveled through South Carolina and Georgia, desperately trying to evade capture. Eventually, the treasure made its way to Washington, Georgia, where Davis met up with them again. In

Washington, Georgia, General Basil Duke took charge of the gold and transferred it into six wagons. But time was running out for the General, and before he could escape, they found themselves surrounded by Union forces. Unable to get away, President Jefferson Davis surrendered himself and the Confederate Treasury in Washington, Georgia.

Uncle Tennessee's cavalry helped take charge of the wagons with orders to transport them to Washington, DC.

In Wilkes County, Georgia, the wagon train was again attacked. This time, by stragglers from both the Union and Confederate armies who had heard of the treasure. The stragglers outnumbered Company M's small force and won the skirmish. They divided up the bounty, stuffing it into any kind of bag they could find and hanging it on their saddles.

The riders stole so much that they were overloaded, stuffing it into their boots and shirts. Some hid their share or discarded large quantities all over Wilkes County. The gold was never found or accounted for.

Just as the story was getting good, Uncle Tennessee, leaning too far back in his porch chair, slipped and darn near fell over. He then took notice that the bottom of the jug was becoming visible. "It's late." he said, "We should hit the hay."

James Tennessee Adams

Chapter 2

Moonlight Marriage – Midnight Murder

The next day, after breakfast, I cut and hung tobacco in our small barn. We had a good crop, and the harvest was just coming to an end. Uncle helped me, and in no time at all, we finished our chores. Afterward, we had some of Mary's fried chicken, okra, beans, and potatoes; then we relaxed on the front porch.

That evening, my wife accompanied me, along with a friend, Mr. Jack Bon, and Uncle Tennessee, on a trip of both business and pleasure. We started out at dusk, I in my magisterial capacity, upon a journey fraught with much happiness, for the two souls I would marry.

Tennessee acted as pilot. After driving the team as far as we could through East Carnegie, until there was no road left, the four of us climbed down off the wagon. We had a basket of Mary's biscuits and, everybody's favorite, key lime pies, two lanterns, and my bible. Uncle took charge of Topsy and Charlie, the horses that pulled our wagon, tying them to a tree alongside two others. Then, we went by foot down a path, across a deep ravine, and up a steep hill, to the top of a high knob, through a country no one would dare go except to get married or divorced.

Uncle said a lot of folks had built up on this hill so they could live close to town, but avoid city life. Why anyone would choose this time and this place for a wedding is beyond my ability to reason, but many others had made their way there as well. Soon we stood at the door of James Adams's home, Uncle Tennessee's son.

Arriving late, we found the yard full of people. Each family had been asked to bring two lanterns. The lanterns were being hung on the tree limbs of the sawtooth oak trees that surrounded the front of the house. The moon was glowing brightly, and the glimmer from the lanterns, and yellow paper streamers created a magical scene. Altogether, I could see the romantic attraction of a moonlight marriage and was instantly put in the mood for a wedding.

While they waited for me and the bridal party, they spent the time dancing to a banjo and fiddle accompaniment. Neighbors, Skippy Hall, Charlie Brown, and Boo Baysinger, very popular entertainers in these parts, had everyone stepping lively to songs like, "*Skip to My Lou*," and singing, "Hurry up slow poke, do oh do, I'll get her back in spite of you. Gone again, what shall I do, I'll get another girl sweeter than you."

When all was ready, the party drew up in the form of a horseshoe radiating from both sides of the large covered porch.

James, home only two months from the Spanish-American War, wore his uniform. My cousin, Nate, the groom, who had served alongside his father in that war, wore his uniform as well. They looked quite dashing in their dark blue uniforms with a single line of nine silver buttons down the front.

The bride, Miss Mary Livingston, looked very feminine in a white blouse with a stand-up collar edged in lace, a ruffle and lace trimmed front yoke, and a row of tiny buttons at the front bib with elongated cuffs trimmed with ribbon. The couple stood on the porch with the attendants, Miss Tiney Able and Mrs. Sam Sneed, at their sides.

With Mr. Bon behind us, we stood at the center of it all–beneath the open skies, atop a knob, out of sight of civilization. There, with fair lunar shedding her soft beams upon the party and the clock inside ticking unusually loud, as if to make lunatics of us all, I pronounced the ceremony that made one of these loving twain.

After the ceremony, the guests were invited to the large dining room where a huge feast had been prepared. Every good thing was there, and everything there was good.

We joined the others in wishing the newlywed couple a long and happy life.

Mr. Bon drank too much, mumbled an excuse, and found a place to rest.

***

Uncle Tennessee approached me at 11:30 p.m., with his gold watch in his right hand and a glass of whiskey in the other.

"Think we should get a move on, Bob?"

"Yeah, but I haven't seen Mr. Bon in some time," I said.

"He's sleeping it off in the barn. James is going into town in the morning; he can ride along with him." Then he asked, "How long have you known that boy?"

"Not long, about four months."

"What business is he in?"

"He works for the railroad in the telegraph office. He moved to town last June, I believe."

"How is it you became such good friends in such a short time?"

"Well, he's a very agreeable man. Never a harsh word, always engaging and helpful. He does ask a lot of questions, though. That be his only drawback."

"What kinda' questions?" Uncle Tennessee asked.

"He just wants to get to know everyone, I guess. Always asking about this one and that."

Then I noticed a familiar look on Uncle Tennessee's face. He had a way of squinting his blue eyes intensifying his gaze, wrinkling his nose, raising his upper lip, and showing a full set of teeth. It was unnerving and could stop a conversation cold. He was not a man to be toyed with; he could be as gentle as a prayer or as sharp as a dagger. They say he'd never lost a fight, but you'd never hear him say that. Never boastful, prideful, or vain, but he cleaned up every morning and brushed his coat and shoes. Tall and wiry looking, with a handsome bearded face, he walked upright and briskly, like a man going places. A fine figure of a man, and he commanded respect.

"It was a good party, wasn't it?" I said, changing the subject.

"Sure, it was a humdinger."

"Uncle James told me you paid for the whole thing, provided they have a moonlight marriage. Is that so?"

"Yep", he said, "I always fancied a moonlight wedding." He cut me off, saying, "You better find that wife of yorn."

James Wiley Adams' family, Tiner's Hill, Johnson City, Tennessee

I found my Mary talking with the new bride, Mrs. Mary Adams, and her Nate. They seemed to be the happiest couple on earth. My Mary helped with the clean-up and had a basket of things to take home with her. Together, we congratulated the two again and wished them all the best. With that, we began saying our goodbyes to the others and headed for the wagon. Uncle Tennessee took the reins again, and being a jim-dandy teamster, he backed the team up and steered them down the moonlit, shadowy trail towards home.

About a third of the way, he pulled up on the reins and brought the team to a halt. Handing the reins to my wife, he said, "You mind holding this team for a spell while us men make water, Miss Mary?"

Mary, who had been going on about all the baked goods at the party, took hold of the leather straps and nodded. I didn't know what to think as I had no need to go, but figuring Uncle Tennessee wanted me to go with him, I followed.

"What are you thinking, Uncle?" I asked as we walked to the far side of a huge boulder to the right of the trail. It was taller than four men and many times as big around. About the size of a barn, you might say.

"I want to tell you something, Bob. Your family and I want to share with you, but you have to promise never to tell a soul."

"Sure, Unc, but here? Why here?"

"It has to be here and now," he said. "I wanted to do this on the way up, but you had to go and invite that Jack Bon feller. I needed cover to come here because I'm being followed, and I suspect it might be that Bon feller. I think he's a Pinkerton."

"A Pinkerton man? Why would a Pinkerton be following you?"

"Listen up, boy. We don't have time for jawboning; we got work to do. I'm leaving town tomorrow; no one can know where I am going. I'm being followed, and if I'm right, tonight we led the man who has been following me to my son James."

"But Uncle Tennessee, what could you have done to get the Pinkertons after you?" Just when I asked the question, I remembered the note that fell from his pocket and the words, "They're on to you," and put it all together.

"You remember me telling you about all that Confederate gold that disappeared?"

"Yeah, why?"

"Well, it ain't exactly all disappeared."

My mouth opened, but I couldn't speak. I watched as Uncle Tennessee moved his hand around the bottom side of the huge boulder. First, pulling out some brush and some dead wood pressed hard under the rock. Then, he felt around and dug a bit with his hand, pulling away dirt and stones. That's when, to my amazement, he pulled out a sack about the size of a three-pound sack of onions. With the other hand, he pulled out a second sack.

"Help me, boy, this is heavy," Uncle Tennessee said; then he shoved a bag into my hands, which I nearly dropped. It weighed much more than onions. It was heavy, just like a sack of gold. I thought to myself, *I'm holding Confederate gold!* My jaw dropped, and my heart began to race. I was at once rich and an accomplice to a crime. How would I reconcile one with the other?

"Let's go around the other side of this rock and approach the wagon from the rear so your Missus doesn't see what we have. We'll cover it up with the blankets in the back until we get home."

We were both watching Mary to make sure she didn't turn and see us placing the sacks in the wagon under the blankets. We never noticed someone slipping up on us.

"Well, well, boys, what a pleasant surprise," laughed the voice of Jack Bon. "I guess I know why you left me in that barn."

I nearly jumped out of my boots, but Uncle Tennessee looked calm and was getting that scary look on his face. When his eyes squinted, his nose wrinkled, and his upper lip rose, I knew he was not going to stay peaceful.

"Is that what I think it is in those sacks?"

Looking closer, I realized he was holding a gun.

"Why the gun, Jack?"

"Don't play dumb, Bob. I had a hunch your uncle was the man I'd been hunting, but I didn't expect you would be involved. You might hang for that mistake."

"What are you talking about, Jack? I thought we were friends."

"I don't work for the railroad. I work for the Pinkerton Detective Agency, and I'm not here to make friends."

"I had a hunch you would lead me to that gold, old man."

Uncle Tennessee, hearing that, pursed his lips and raised his eyebrow in contempt.

"Your momma didn't teach you respect, did she?" Uncle Tennessee said, not expecting an answer.

"Well, if you don't respect your elders, I'll have to teach you." With that, Uncle Tennessee grabbed the gun by the barrel with his left hand, shoving it to his right and down at the same time, hitting Jack with a powerful right. The two of them wrestled, turning around and around, each trying to get the better of the other. Uncle Tennessee forced the gun up in the air above their heads and to the left and again punched Jack with a crushing right fist. Bon was a lot younger than Unc and clearly used to scrapping. He, being shorter and stocky, was hard to move off his feet. I was getting ready to jump in when I heard the thunder of Uncle's Colt 45 and saw Jack Bon drop like a rock. Uncle Tennessee had a look of astonishment on his face.

When I turned, I saw Mary holding Uncle Tennessee's 45. Not wanting to carry his gun at the wedding, he had left it in its holster near the driver's seat.

"Mary, what have you done?" I yelled.

"Nobody's hanging my husband," she said in a quiet voice.

"My God, what have we gotten ourselves into?"

"No big deal, Bob, he's just a Pinkerton. They're not much count," Tennessee said.

"But they will come looking for him!" I said.

"Yeah, they will come, but they won't find him," Uncle said. "They never found the gold, did they? We'll bury him in the same hole. They'll come looking for me, but they won't find me either. I'm leaving town."

"What about the gold?" I asked.

"I'll leave that with you and James to divide. I would never be able to spend any of it anyhow."

After burying the body, we once again mounted our carriage and headed home.

Mary was uncharacteristically quiet. Uncle Tennessee sought to ease her mind, saying, "You did what you had to do, Miss Mary. Family gotta stick together. That Bon feller coulda' hung us all."

Mary just stared straight ahead, silent for the entire ride home.

"You say you're leaving, Uncle. Where will you go?" I asked.

"A little place about fifty miles north. I have a job there working for a feller, but you didn't hear that. Don't breathe a word to anyone about it. It will take them a long time to find me up that way. You and James divide up the gold and help the family with it. I know if I need anything, you'll take care of me. I'm too old to need much. Never had nothin' much, and I'm used to it."

19

Chapter 3

Call to Worship

C ome the morning, we were all up early. Mary, still quiet, put the coffee on to perk, then set out some biscuits on a plate. Uncle brushed his coat like nothing had ever happened.

"You headin' out this morning, Uncle?" I said.

"Later," he said. "First we gotta' go to church."

"Church?" I knew he could hear the astonishment in my voice.

"It's Sunday, ain't it? Never miss church for nothin'."

"I don't know, Uncle, I don't feel much like going to church after last night."

"Maybe we should talk, son. Last night was an unpleasant piece of business, but we did what we had to. I believe the good Lord was with us, that He saw' what was done, and it was us He protected. Now, today is the Lord's day, and I'll be giving Him His day."

"But, Uncle, don't you feel bad for that man?"

"Yes, I do! And we can pray for his everlasting soul here, or we can do it in church, where we belong. Bob," he said, "I spent four long years in the saddle, killing good men. My Captain raised his sword, and the bugler sounded the charge.

That's when I knew what had to be done. My country ordered me to kill, not God. Smoke filled the air. The smell of powder, the sound of galloping horses, and at times, we could hear shots whizzing past our heads, but we kept moving forward. Once, we were in the thick of battle. I was slashing my way through the enemy with my sword. I guess I could've killed six men that day. All of a sudden, a minie ball hit me. It took me clean off my horse, and I thought I was a goner. When I came to, I found the ball had struck the coat pocket over my heart. Hurt like the dickens! I reached inside that pocket and found a Christian medallion my wife gave me. I'd stuck it in my pocket, and it saved my life. You see, Bob, man has his law and God's got His. No one knows whose side God was on in that war. Plenty of good men got killed on both sides, who should never have died. I think God protected me because of that medallion. Because I carried it, He knew I had accepted Him as my savior. No matter whether I did right or wrong, as long as I gave my heart to Jesus, God took care of me. Now that Bon fella, he didn't come up to me and say give me that money and you can go free. If he had, I'd have gladly give it to him and been shed of it. No, he was just lookin' for someone to throw into jail and make himself look good. Jail would have separated you and me from our families that need us. And why? When I grabbed that gold, I only had a second to think about it. It was either I took it, or someone else did—so I took it! I have regretted it ever since, but giving it back was never an option. It didn't belong to them, stealing it. And it didn't belong to them up there in Washington either. In four years, I never saw one of them

Washington people in the saddle next to me when I was getting' shot at. It's like this, Bob: you're a magistrate–folks come before you, and you decide whether they done right or done wrong. But ya gotta' remember, there are two kinds of law. There is the letter of the law, and the spirit of the law."

"I don't follow, Uncle."

"Well, the letter of the law tells you not to steal. But the spirit of the law tells you why they created the law in the first place. They created that law to protect folks. That gold didn't belong to anyone, the way I saw it. I may have broken the letter of the law, but I didn't break the spirit of it. And if you don't violate the reason for the law, then the law don't matter no how. Do you understand what I'm trying to tell you?"

"Uncle, I'm gonna have to think on it. I'll go hitch up the team now."

Together, we headed for the old Sinking Creek Baptist Church. Uncle Tennessee, wanting to break the silence, spoke first. "This church is the oldest in the state, built in 1772. It was closed down during the war. Reckon there weren't nobody left to go."

Sinking Creek Baptist Church

"In 1869, Sinking Creek reorganized the Watauga Association. And that association, right here in 1772, gave us the first majority-rule system of American democracy. So right here on this land, the Articles established an independent government, separate from the United States, based on democracy, as we know it today. And they done it four long years before Thomas Jefferson wrote the American Declaration of Independence."

"By Joe, there's been a lot of history made right here in these mountains."

Coming up on the church, Uncle Tennessee said, "We put a new roof on the church last year. We all pitched in."

I just nodded my head, not ready to talk.

Arriving at the church early, Tennessee took care of the team while Mary and I went inside. The Reverend Donald Smithbaugher met us with a big smile and a welcome handshake. He was a tall man with short-cropped hair and a large chin.

"How you doin', Reverend?" I said.

Mary just smiled and curtsied, not feeling talkative either.

"Doin' right nice, Robert, right nice. Great to see you, good people out today. Especially good to see your Uncle Tennessee. He has done so much for our little church. This new roof was really needed."

"So, Uncle was the one who donated the money for the roof?"

"Ah, yeah. I thought you knew, Robert." I shouldn't have said. I was supposed to keep it quiet, but I thought you knew."

"No problem, I'll keep it between us, Reverend."

"Thanks, Robert. I speak too quickly sometimes. Well, have a seat anywhere; we should have a full house this morning, the weather being warm and all."

Uncle Tennessee came in eventually and sat down next to Mary and me. The service was a good one for giving comfort to sinners. I thought it was appropriate, and it had a calming effect. After the service, we made our way to the wagon. The sun shone brightly and warmed us.

I helped Mary up and climbed up behind her. Uncle was having a conversation with our horses, Topsy and Charlie. He liked to remind the horses that they were appreciated. He always had something to give them, whether it be an apple or a handful of oats–a habit he began in the Cavalry, no doubt. Then, he jumped up on the wagon and took the reins. Tipping our hats to the others while leaving, we moved down the road toward home.

An Old Soldier

Uncle Tennessee left Johnson City in the morning, like he said he would. He left behind, his first wife, Louisa Jane, along with his home and all his possessions. There was a lot of talk about where he might have disappeared to, but no one had seen hide nor hair of him. Louisa Jane (Orr) filed for divorce after a few years, citing abandonment.

Ten years passed without anyone hearing from Uncle Tennessee. He had been running a gristmill in Sticklyville, Virginia, and had carved out a new life for himself. He married again, this time to a lady by the name of Rebecca (Hammer) Adams. When she passed away, he married a third time, to Amanda J. (Cox) Christy.

Uncle Tennessee returned to Johnson City a much older man. His attitude and vigor were gone; all he had left was his will to live, and it was weak. The law no longer cared, and nobody was following.

In 1920, he was admitted into the National Home for Disabled Volunteer Soldiers in Washington County,

Tennessee. He was treated at the *Mountain Branch Home for Disabled Volunteer Soldiers Veterans' Hospital*, also known as the *National Soldiers' Home*, where he died on August 21, 1924.

James Tennessee Adams, sitting with son Tom, standing

Uncle Tennessee was laid to rest in his blue Cavalry uniform. Many family and friends attended the funeral: Mary and I, Nate and his Mary, Tennessee's third wife, Amanda J. (Cox) Christy, his son, James; James's daughter, Temperance ("Tempy"); and her husband, Pet DeLoach. Tempy's firstborn, seven-year-old daughter, Macel DeLoach, made five generations attending the funeral. Macel stood on her tiptoes to peek into the casket, and the sight of her great-grandfathers lifeless body, and long white beard, scared her.

Uncle Tennessee had a military funeral on August 22, at the *Veterans Mountain Home National Cemetery,* where little Macel, fidgeting around, nearly fell into the grave. Other than those distractions, it was a somber and tearful event.

My uncle's passing marked the end of a way of life. Nothing would ever be quite the same. He had been a strong head of the family and an anchor that kept us from drifting away from our roots. Even during his long absence, he was never out of our hearts. It was always, "What would Uncle do?" His strong hand and positive philosophy of life were instilled in each of us. Uncle's love and affection always showed through in everything he did, even with his sharpest command. And his favorite saying was, "Never turn agin' ur own." His faith in God guided him even when others could not understand his actions. He seemed to understand life better than most. He always knew what had to be done and never doubted himself.

The loss of this tough, no-nonsense patriarch left a void no individual could fill. Slowly, each of us picked up the pieces and, applying the lessons learned, developed our own approach to life based on his model and directives. This especially meant living by his adage: "Never turn against your own."

Family took on more significance than ever. We grew closer than I thought possible. At times, I thought the family alone might fill the Sinking Creek Baptist Church on Sundays.

Uncle Tennessee left his mark on the world. He came into it like everyone else, but with a powerful faith in himself and drive, he motivated others to do more. He had loyally served his country, his family, and his church. We came to trust and believe in him. And if his strong belief was enough, we can be sure he has gone to be with the angels.

Cousin James, Mary, and I never talked about Jack Bon again. We continued to live simply, secure in the knowledge that the money was there if needed. We used some to build a home for Uncle Tennessee's grandson, Nate Adams, and his wife, Mary. They built it atop a steep hill, on a high knob surrounded by other knobs, through a country no one would dare go to, except to get married or divorced.

Chapter 4

Haunted by the Past

e awoke to a bright, sunny day—one of those days when everything feels right and nothing can go wrong.

I washed and prepared for the day. Mary brought me a steaming cup of coffee. I took it out on the porch and wondered at the sunlight glistening through the early morning fog, while listening to a mockingbird, as she cooked up a mess of pork chops, biscuits, gravy, and eggs. Joining my wife at the table, I ate without regard for my growing middle, heaping an extra bit of Mary's strawberry jam on the still-warm, freshly baked biscuits. The smell was delightful.

An hour later, I was at my office on Buffalo Street, in downtown Johnson City, the better area of town, with a storefront to be proud of. I had been fortunate. I was able to afford an office that was so nice and so well-located. I had just hung a new shingle, **Robert Baily, District Magistrate**. I worked hard for everything, and the State of Tennessee had been good to me.

Across the street, my cousin Macel worked as a waitress at Lacey's Restaurant, near the Windsor Hotel.

Inside my office, I marked the date on the calendar hanging on the wall, as was my custom, August 9, 1935. It was

8:30 a.m. before my secretary, Lolly Tubs, rushed through the door. Not like her to be late, I gave her and my good silver pocket watch a hard look.

"Good morning, Bob," she said. "Sorry, I'm running late. I stopped to get you the *Johnson City Comet,* and the owner, old Glenn Stroup, would not stop gabbing."

"What was he so talkative about? You usually can't get a word out of him," I said.

"Something about a murder. He was talking to the clerk, Jimmy Mathis, about it. I didn't have time to read it. Here, take the paper while I see what's on our schedule." I took the paper, half-irritated and half-curious, unfolding it as I moved toward my desk. Then, the headline hit me like a punch in the gut:

MISSING PINKERTON MAN FOUND MURDERED

My legs immediately felt shaky and weak. I sank heavily into my leather armchair, the paper trembling in my hands. My eyes scanned the rest of the story, each word weighing heavier than the last.

Sheriff Miles Gordon filed a report today, stating the body found near Tiner's Hill was indeed that of missing Pinkerton Detective Jack Bon, who disappeared on October 17th, 1898.

The sheriff said, "Young Dennis Baysinger of 1724 West Eleventh Street, Johnson City, was coon hunting on the moonlit night of August 1. He and his dog, Digger, had sat down to rest against a huge boulder just off the road to Tiner's Hill and fell asleep. Dennis, or Beanie as he is called, said that when he awoke, he saw where his dog had been digging. There, the full moon gleamed off the bones of a man, now identified as the missing Detective."

Suspecting foul play, the sheriff's office had the site carefully excavated to preserve evidence. The complete skeletal remains were found, along with a Pinkerton detectives' badge and a single lead slug, which the sheriff said was most likely the cause of death.

My breath hitched, and the page blurred before my eyes. I could almost feel the ghost of Jack Bon standing there in my office, his shadow stretching across the years and the safe distance I thought I'd put between us.

The sheriff had no suspects in the murder and no leads to go on. After contacting the Pinkerton Detective Agency, he learned Jack Bon had been employed by them at the time of his disappearance and was investigating persons of interest, in connection with the lost Confederate gold shipment from 1865.

Now, it seemed he wasn't the only thing unearthed that moonlit night. Memories, buried as deeply as his body, clawed their way to the surface.

The sheriff lamented, "That missing gold could be worth five hundred million dollars. How or why it would have any connection to Johnson City is not clear at this time. The gold was thought to have been stolen from a small federal force, charged with conveying it to Washington, D.C., towards the end of the War Between the States. It had been attacked by a band of renegades from both sides and carried off. No trace of it has ever been found. It is the most enduring mystery of the war."

As I read the words, I felt my stomach churn and a lump in my throat develop. I couldn't continue reading. In my mind, I knew what we had done was wrong, but there was no way of correcting any of it. I could not—I would not—turn on my own family. That would never happen. But now, after all these years, our deeds had come back to haunt us. I wondered what would come of us now.

Rising to my feet, I said, "I'm not feeling well. Cancel all my appointments. I'm going home." I had to talk to my cousin James. Outside, I leaped into my 1934 Model 40B Ford I had purchased four months earlier. Pressing the floor starter, it fired up immediately. I pushed gently on the gas pedal and headed down Market Street towards Tiner's Hill. As I drove closer, I saw the Sheriff's Deputies, Junior Graham and Tom Boy Figley, parked on the left side of the road in a familiar location. I did not slow down but pressed on. My business was more urgent than ever.

The road had since been extended, allowing me to drive all the way to the house. The old days were gone. It was the modern era. But all the modern conveniences could not take us away from the news that seemed like a million years ago.

As I pulled up to the house where I married Nate and Mary so long ago, I saw James coming from the barn where he was probably doing the morning milking. As I strode over toward him, I asked, "Have you heard the news, James?"

"What news?" he asked.

"It's in the morning paper, James. They found a body. The body of a missing detective."

"Calm yourself, Bob, and tell me what you heard?" James said.

Clutching the paper in my right hand, I passed it to him. James sat down on a stump near the pigpen, pulled out his spectacles, and started reading.

"Yeah, this is bad, Bob. But we have to keep our cool."

"But James, they're gonna learn he was tracking Uncle Tennessee; then they will come asking us questions. I'm worried about my Mary."

"Nothing is going to happen fast, but when it does, you just have to remember, you don't know nothin'! No matter what they ask, or how many times they ask it, we don't know nothin'!" He slammed his open hand against his leg. "Go home, Bob, and tell your Mary. Tell her not to worry. Everything will be okay."

"Alright, I'll be back tomorrow," I said.

I felt better after talking to James, but I still had to tell Mary. All the way home, I kept going over the events of that evening. Every word and every move haunted me. It pained me to think of it, but I could think of nothing else. When I pulled the Model T into the yard, Mary came out to greet me. I had a hard time telling her, but I remained calm. Afterward, I told her that James said not to worry. She became quiet again, just like that night, and we held each other for a long time.

Tailored Weaves & Tangled Webs

The next morning dawned just like the day before, but there was no joy in it. Sleep had come hard and did not last. And neither of us was hungry. I left for work early, maybe hoping by doing so the end of our nightmare might come sooner. At noon, I left again for James's house to see if he had any ideas.

Arriving at James's, I was surprised to find he had company: my very beautiful cousin, Temperance, and her husband, Pet DeLoach. They had moved from Johnson City to Greeneville, Tennessee, some months back, with their four daughters, Macel, Bessie, Leona, and Evelyn. There, they purchased a small farm on Middle Creek Road, where Pet raised tobacco and corn.

Macel had moved to Greeneville with them, but she didn't like farm life. She told me how the neighbor, Albert Nahar, one day gave her a white horse. When she told her dad about it, he was suspicious. He knew that fellow pretty good, and he never gave anything away. The next morning, they went out to the barn and found the horse standing up, leaning against the wall. He had died standing up. Her daddy told her, "That's why he gave you the horse, so we would have to bury it for him." Macel always laughed when she told that story, but at the time, she was very angry. Feisty as ever, the 5'2" Macel, marched right over to the neighbors and told Mr. Nahar, "Shame on you for tricking me like that." She said the 6'2" Mr. Nahar, finding her amusing, apologized and offered to handle the funeral arrangements.

Eighteen-year-old Macel decided farm life wasn't for her. She wanted to go back to work at Lacey's Restaurant in Johnson City, so Tempy and Pet drove her back.

Julia Temperance Adams & husband, Pet DeLoach

Macel would stay with Nate and Mary and, like them, needed to be told what was happening, as they were sure to be questioned.

After Tempy and Pet left, the rest of us sat down in the parlor to a lunch of ham and bean soup with cornbread. Having skipped breakfast, I was quite ready for something.

While eating, we tossed around our thoughts.

Macel had an interesting question.

"How would the Pinkertons, or anyone else, know my great-grandpa had taken that gold? Or if he did, how much?"

"Well," James said, "they couldn't. Nobody could. They were speculatin' he might have. But Bon died the night of our Nate's moonlit marriage. They could learn he was here, and my daddy, Tennessee, was here, and the next day they were both gone. That is suspicious looking."

I said, "Yes, and if they suspect Uncle, suspicion will fall on the rest of us. And that could be dangerous."

"One thing about it: they can think what they want, but they can't prove a damned thing–unless one of us squawk," James said.

"That's sure enough right, James," I said, "But we still need to figure something out because our reputation is at risk."

Macel said, "None of us took it, and none of us spent any of it. And it never belonged to the Federal Government anyhow, so why should they have it?"

"Let's not forget a man died on account of it," I said.

"Yeah, Bob, but don't forget a lot of soldiers on both sides died for it, too. I don't know that it's justifiable, but those others were honorable men and had just as much right to live," James said.

"We'll just have to think on it a bit more," Bob said. "There must be a way to divert attention away from us."

PART II

Macel

Chapter 5

The Pen-pal and The Cover-up

James Wiley Adams & Wife Sarafine Orr

James and Sarafine were married on November 15, 1874. Sarafine's father was from England, and her mother was full-blooded Cherokee Indian. She was built solid, wore her hair up in a bun, and never seemed to stop working. When she spoke, her eyes brightened, and her warm heart showed through. She seemed content and eager to make everyone comfortable. Pouring James a cup of freshly perked coffee, she warned, "It's hot!"

Spilling a little over into his saucer, he sipped it from there. Pushing his chair back from the table, he turned to Macel. "When you gonna get married, girl?"

"Well, I'm not. Leastways, not soon, Poppa."

"You got a boyfriend?"

"No, but I have a pen-pal, does that count?" she said, laughing.

"A pen-pal, what's that?"

"Oh, cousin James Farrin works up in Pennsylvania. He came home to visit once and gave me this fella's name. He told me to write him. We been a writin' for two years now, but I don't spect' I'll ever see him. He's too far away."

"That's kinda funny. Only you would have the daring to write a complete stranger. Well, I hope you and that pen-pal work out, even if he is a Yankee."

***

Two days passed before Sheriff Miles Gordon showed up at my office. "Bob, I need to ask you some questions about this murder investigation."

"Go ahead, Sheriff."

"You were friends with Jack Bon, right?"

"Yeah, sorta."

"Didn't you find it a little odd, him disappearing overnight?"

"Yes, I did, Sheriff, but I just figured he was ordered by the railroad to move on. Only knew him for a few months, ya know. Ain't like we were real close."

"The last time he was seen alive was at your cousin Nate's wedding. Did you see him that night?"

"Well, yeah, he was there."

"Did you know he was following your uncle, Tennessee?"

"No, I didn't. Why would he? My uncle was a good man. He had an honorable war record and was never arrested for anything." I retorted, clearly irritated, "I won't stand for anyone disparaging my uncle's good name, Sheriff!"

"Calm down, Bob, I just need to ask." The questioning went on and on until it was clear the Adams were the only suspects. After me, he talked to James and Nate, and then he was back again, asking more questions.

After a few days, we all met at James's place.

James said, "Guess we've all been drilled by that Miles Gordon. He's a tenacious son of a bitch, ain't he? Like a damn pit bull on moonshine."

"He sure enough is!" replied Nate.

I said, "All that money ain't worth nuthin' if you can't spend it. And we'll always have that Sheriff to worry about now."

"Well," James said, "all we gotta do is keep bein' a dead end to that sheriff. If he talks to enough dead ends, he'll quit his askin'. But ur right about that money. It ain't nothin' but a worry havin' it around."

Nate changed the subject, asking Macel if she'd heard from her pen pal.

"I sure did. My cousin James Farrin came by last evening and brought that fella with him. There I was in an old dress and bare feet, listening to the radio, when James knocked at the door. Then he just stood there with that simple grin on his face, not sayin' nothin'. Then I noticed a man behind him in the dark, and from his picture, I knew it was him. I nearly died."

"Well, I'll bet that was a shock. What was he like?" Sarafine asked.

"He was a real nice gentleman. The three of us visited for a long while, listenin' to the radio and talkin', and then they left. This morning, they stopped again and said they were going to drive over to Greeneville to meet my parents."

"That sounds serious."

"I hope so," Macel whispered with a wide-eyed grin.

***

The Tale of a Loving Twain

Two days later, James noticed a 1932 Ford four-door sedan he had never seen before at Nate's place, so he went to investigate. He found me, James Farrin, and my pen pal, Clarence, loading up some of my things.

"Where you goin'?" he said.

"Hi, Poppa," I said, giving him a big hug around the neck. "I want you to meet someone."

"Poppa, this here is my new husband, Clarence."

"Your husband! When did this happen? Why wasn't I told?"

Clarence was tall with black hair and light blue eyes. The eyes conveyed both a welcome and a caution. Standing erect, he wore a big smile. He had a personal magnetism and hands that showed he was no stranger to hard work.

"Now, Poppa, we didn't have time for a big doin's because Clarence has to be back to work in Pennsylvania tomorrow. So, we went downtown to Buffalo Street yesterday, and Justice of the Peace D. Pearce married us right then and there."

Clarence extended his hand and said, "I'm proud to meet you, sir."

"Young man, you'd better take good care of my granddaughter, you hear? She means an awful lot to me."

"I promise I will, sir. I'll take good care of her."

"And bring her back as often as you can, would ya?"

"Yes, sir! I will do that."

"Stop over to the barn before you go," James said. "I have something for you."

After we finished loading a few things into Clarence's car, we headed to James's place.

"You two go inside and have a coffee with your grandmother before you leave. I'll be along," James said.

Inside, I introduced Clarence, and we had coffee. Before long, Grandpa James came in and sat down.

"I put some things in the back of your car, under the spare tire. Don't open it till you get home."

Looking into Clarence's eyes, he said, "It's just some gardening tools Macel always liked. She loves to garden, you know?"

"I'm sure gonna miss you, little one," James said.

"You're a bold one and spirited, just like your great-grandpap, Tennessee. He loved new adventures and never let anything hold him back."

I just smiled and hugged his neck.

"I'll miss you too, Poppa!"

"Well, we'd better go now," Clarence said. "We have a long way to go."

Before they left, Nate and Mary came. Bob showed up just in time to wave goodbye.

We made it to Beaver Falls, Pennsylvania, late and stayed in the apartment Clarence shared with Jim Farrin, since Jim was not there. The next day, after work, Clarence and I went to look at a house for rent on 11th Street. It was located on the edge of town, and it had property with it. We signed the papers right there and took possession. That evening, after moving a couch, a bed, and some chairs in from the apartment, we slept in our own home.

The next day, I remembered something Poppa had whispered in my ear as he hugged me goodbye.

"Careful, little one, those garden tools are just for you and no one else. You take care of them." I didn't know what he meant, but after Clarence returned home, I went to the car and lifted the spare tire to find a burlap sack and quickly hid it in my garden shed.

Macel & Clarence on their wedding day

Meeting all of Clarence's family and trying to remember their names was a chore. His mom and dad, Marie and Bert, had twelve children. Clarence was the oldest. After him came Edna, Lawrence, Bertha, Robert, Betty, David, Vince, Harry,

Eddie, Marie, and Dorothy. They were a close-knit bunch. All were workers and always ready to have a good time together. We saw each other often and enjoyed a close relationship.

I worked day and night, until I had that house looking and feeling like a home. We borrowed curtains and bought used furniture for the living room and kitchen. At night, we took walks down the main street of town, and I was surprised at how many people he knew. He was proud of his new wife and took every opportunity to introduce me. Everyone struggled with my name. They called me Marcel, Mazel, and Macelli, and they rarely said it right. He often told folks he took me out of the hills of Tennessee and would teasingly say, "She never had shoes on her feet until I married her." I'd playfully swat him and say, "You big liar, you."

But I didn't mind. I just smiled. Everyone had fun with my southern accent. It was a whole new adventure. It was my new world, and I was going to enjoy it.

One evening, while reading the paper at the kitchen table, Clarence said, "There have been a couple of robberies in town. We'd better keep our eyes open."

"Where would you hide something valuable in this house?" I asked.

Clarence answered laughingly, "That makes me think of something funny. My mom and dad made moonshine for years. I sold it and delivered it to just about everyone in town. "One afternoon, I was making deliveries in the downtown area. I was parked on the hill near the Rialto Theater on the main street of town. The trunk of my car was full of booze. It was hot, and just when I stepped out of the car onto the sidewalk, Big John, a police officer, stepped out of the alley. We knew each other pretty well and were friends, but he was still the law, and I didn't want him to know what I was up to. I moved as we talked to get farther away from my car. Just when I thought we were far enough away, and I would get away with it, the sweltering heat of the day caused some of the jugs in the back to pop their lids. Moonshine trickled out and ran down the curb right beside us. Big John either didn't see it or pretended not to, but I thought I was in big trouble. When I told my brother Lawrence about it, we had a good laugh. The cops must have raided our home a half dozen times looking for moonshine, but they never found anything."

"Where did you hide it?" I asked excitedly.

"Mom hid it in the garden, in mason jars buried beside the potato plants."

"That's so funny. And they never found any?"

"Nope, they knew he had it, but they could never find any. Nobody ever looked in the garden."

Laughing uncontrollably, I said, "I declare, that is the funniest thing I ever did hear."

The next day, I worked outside. I cleaned the garden shed and went downtown to buy paint for it. When Clarence came home from work, I told him what I wanted to do.

"Macel, I'm tired!" Clarence said.

"I know you work hard all day in that nasty steel plant, but winter is coming, and we have to be ready for it. There are some things I can't do myself. We just have to work a little longer." Then I said, "See those old used chairs I bought?" Clarence nodded.

"Well, I'm fixin to put some nails in that there wall, and hang them chairs up. We have work to do, and we don't need no chairs till the work is done.

My tenacity, along with my accent, always made Clarence laugh out loud.

"Okay," he said. "What do you want done?"

"I want that garden turned over and some manure for it. I want a three-foot high fence put around that there garden to keep the rabbits out. I'm gonna have it all laid out and fertilized for the spring plantin'."

Energized by her drive, he went out and began turning the ground over. "The neighbor has chickens; maybe he will let me have some manure to mix into the soil," he said. It wasn't long before we had the whole garden laid out, and over the next few weeks, he built the fence and whitewashed it.

In the spring, I planted and tended the garden while Clarence worked at the steel mill. In the evenings, we sometimes walked down the main street, which bustled with shoppers until 9:00 p.m., or met friends for coffee at one of the many restaurants.

Every summer, Clarence kept his promise and took me back to Tennessee to visit. The police investigation there came to a complete halt, just like Poppa said it would, when no evidence could be found. Every fall, we harvested everything in the garden and canned most of it for the winter. It was the life of one who lived modestly but happily.

Macel's Dilemma

It was a warm spring afternoon; Clarence walked through the door just like every other day. Sitting at the kitchen table, he bent over and began removing his work boots. His socks, which were white when he left that morning, were now the color of the dirt floor in the mill. Dirt fell from the cuffs in his work pants as he unlaced and removed his shoes.

"What's for supper?" he asked.

"Fried chicken, mashed potatoes, gravy, and green beans," I said, setting a cup of coffee in front of him.

"I'm sick of that plant, Macel," he said, his voice heavy with frustration. "You can't move up the ladder unless you wear a cross around your neck. I've been passed over for promotion three times now. I have had it up to here with management," he said, pointing his index finger to his neck. "I want to buy a truck and machine so I can work for myself. I've been talking to people, and I think I can make money."

"Do you know how to do that kind of work?" I asked.

"I worked on a farm, and I can do plenty. I can learn what I don't know as I go."

"Why don't you do it? You're too good for that dirty old mill anyhow."

"Well, it will take money. Money, I don't have right now."

"How much will you need?" I said

"Probably a couple of thousand to get started."

"Well," I said, "we have some savings, but not enough. We'll have to figure out how to get the rest if you really want this."

"I do, Macel. I really want this!"

Knowing I was behind him made Clarence's boring job easier to bear. That support put a spring back in his step, long worn down by the grind of his old job. Excited at the prospect of something new, he spent his spare time thinking of possible customers and learning how to charge for hauling coal by the ton. Just six days after our talk, Clarence came home with some news. "There's a truck for sale up the road," he said, his voice buzzing with excitement. "I looked it over, and it'd be perfect for hauling coal. I've got a plan: I'll buy coal from a couple of small mines and make deliveries to homes and stores in town."

"Every home and business uses coal to heat with," Clarence said, his voice brimming with confidence. "Every chimney that belches smoke is burning coal. There is work everywhere."

"How much do they want for that truck, Clarence?"

"It's a 1930 Ford, and he is asking $800."

I gave a slight smile and looked intently into his blue eyes.

"You really want that truck, don't you?"

"Yes, I think we can make money with it. Hell, I know everyone in town. It won't be hard to find business."

I set a cup of coffee in front of him before walking into the other room. When I returned, I took his hand in mine.

"I'm fixin' to tell you something important," I said softly, "but you have to promise you'll never tell a living soul."

Clarence furrowed his brow. "I don't understand, Macel. What do you mean?"

"I mean you have to promise or I ain't telling you."

His gaze met mine, steady and unwavering. "Okay, of course not, I promise."

Without another word, I opened my hand and let six heavy coins drop into his palm. They clinked against each other as they landed. "This is for you. Go over there and buy that truck." Clarence's eyes widened as he inspected the coins. Looking up at me, he exclaimed, "This is gold, Macel. Where did you get this?"

"Poppa gave it to me when we left Tennessee. If that's not enough, there is more."

"More! How much more?" he shouted.

"I don't know. Several jars."

"Jars! Where do you keep jars of gold?"

Seeing how excited he was getting, I decided to tell him the whole story so that he would calm down.

"Listen, Clarence, this is a gift from Poppa, but it is as much a curse as it is a blessing. We cannot use it as we please." I told him the whole story. "So, you see, everyone who has touched this gold could go to jail. Only after everyone involved has passed can the story truly be told. Then, and only then, the next to possess it will have that option. They can tell the whole world about it and give it back, or they can keep it. That's not us. We can never speak of it or use it without great caution."

Clarence, understanding the weight of it, knew I was right, and the two of us kept that secret for the rest of our lives, never telling a soul, until one afternoon in July of 2008.

PART III

Little Joe

Chapter 6

A Family's Legacy

Being the youngest of six, I always saw my parents as normal–ordinary in every way, except for their work ethic. Work was the center of our lives. No baseball, horseback riding, or fishing–not even a board game for diversion. Work was everything, the reason to rise, eat, and go to bed. If we were cold, we were told that the heat was in the tools. "Work harder, and your body will generate its own heat." If we were tired, it was, "Keep going- it'll make you strong." It was also the cure for idleness and boredom. Work was the thing you should be most proud of and the thing most worthy of your time.

They called their firstborn Sonny because of his pleasant disposition. Mom sometimes called him Sunshine. Next came Pet, named after one of our grandfathers. My father taught them to drive trucks and operate heavy equipment. People in town remembered seeing them behind the wheel of a big dump truck, at fourteen, their heads barely visible above the steering wheel.

They started out delivering coal to local businesses. They would back the truck up to the building, lower the metal coal chutes into the window or opening, and shovel whole truckloads of coal by hand. It was back-breaking work, but they didn't give it a second thought. It was just work, and work was good.

Then came my brother James, followed by my sister Patricia. By this time, Dad had started buying heavy equipment and doing excavating work. Sonny and Pet ran the high lifts, while Jim operated the backhoe, installing French drains and sewer lines. Patricia delivered pipes and materials to the job sites using a pickup. Everybody worked together, and everybody played together. In the early years, play consisted of Sonny playing guitar on the front porch and singing, with the rest of us chiming in. Everyone was impressed by his ability to sing loudly, switching effortlessly between a natural pitch and a high falsetto. He called it yodeling, and it was very popular with country singers back then. I learned to do it a bit myself after listening to him long enough.

After Patricia came my brother Earl and, two years later, me. Mom liked to call me Little Joe, like the youngest son on the TV show Ponderosa. By then, Dad had expanded the business into scrapping automobiles. He bought junk cars, compressed them with an H-D9 high lift, and hauled them to a shredder on a refabricated car carrier. He welded a heavy metal hinge to the center of the high-lift bucket and attached a four-inch, thick-walled steel pipe to it. Heavy chains secured the pipe, and at its end, he hung a short chain with a massive hook. My job was to use the high lift to sort the cars and set fire to them, twelve at a time. Once they'd burned down, I'd thread a heavy chain through the driver's side window and out the other, hooking them together. We used the high-lift to crush the cars down to about two or three feet high. When the truck returned from the scrapyard, we'd use the high-lift and hook system to load the flattened cars onto the trailer.

It was a clever idea that my dad developed. No one else was doing it, and it was very profitable. Dad, Earl, and I would do the work, and the work shaped us. It made us tough and kept us off the streets and out of trouble. At sixteen, while my friends complained about mowing postage-stamp-sized lawns, I was driving tractor-trailers and loading them myself with a high-lift.

***

In high school, the football coach asked me to join the team, so I did. But when I told my father that I needed to go after supper to lift weights and practice, he had other plans. "There's a truckload of cement blocks that needs unloading," he said. "You unload that trailer, and you'll be able to whip anyone on the team."

I knew then that my football days were over. My father didn't believe in sports; he believed in work.

I remember vividly the day my father said that he was not going to work seven days a week any longer. "From now on," he said, "I'm only going to work six." He died that year. A massive heart attack took his life at fifty-two, just before I turned seventeen.

Several years later, tragedy struck again when my brother, Pet, passed away from a brain aneurysm. Seven years after that,

Mom fell ill. I spent a lot of time with her, driving back and forth to the hospital and fixing things at home so she would be comfortable. During this time, we talked often. I began asking questions about her life, our family, and her memories. I realized that once she was gone, the stories of our family history would be lost forever.

I asked her about my grandparents, their families, and how she met my dad. That's when my interest in genealogy began. She told me about our ancestors, and I, using the Internet, began to gather information. I sent requests to the National Archives in Washington, D.C., for military records and visited graveyards, gathering as much information as possible. She helped and began to enjoy the detective work with me. We were a team working to uncover the mysteries of a family, and in doing so, we became closer.

Mom's medical problems grew worse. But every day, she cleaned her home, and before she retired, she made certain there were no dishes left dirty in the sink.

"Why do you worry about those few dishes? Why not do that in the morning?" Her answer was pure Mom: "If I die in my sleep, I want my house to be clean when they come to get me." Always, it was your work you took pride in.

***

Then one day, we found ourselves in the Emergency Room. It looked like the end.

"Little Joe," she called me affectionately, "come closer."

"What is it, Mom?"

"I want to tell you where the money is to bury me."

"You're not going to die, Mom. I won't let that happen."

"Hush up and listen! In my safe, there is a little red purse. Inside, you will find what cash I have and directions. Follow them closely."

Mom was gone within the hour. Overwhelmed with grief, I did exactly as she instructed. She had everything planned just like she said, with the money set aside and her wishes clearly outlined.

It wasn't long after that my brother Sonny fell ill to cancer and passed away. Shortly thereafter, his son Biff also died. Loss seemed relentless. My nephew Ronnie, my cousins Patty and Tom, my sister in-law Jan, and then my brother James, all gone.

Earl had moved to Phoenix, and my sister Jean was battling lung cancer. Her recovery was fraught with complications from the radiation and chemo. She suffered terribly with one setback after another until she stopped wanting to live. I did everything I could to help her, but her pain consumed her.

After one exceptionally grueling day, I started going through my mom's safe. It brought back sad memories. Everything was just as I had left it, along with a few extra things I had added, like the visitation book from the funeral home.

Then, I spotted something I had not seen before: an envelope addressed to me. It stood upright, pressed tightly against the right side, taped to the wall. I completely overlooked it after my mother's passing. Trembling, I opened it with unsteady hands. Inside, I found a letter addressed to me, and slowly, I began to read.

"In the garden," the letter began, "buried in jars beside where the potatoes once grew, there is some money. Inside one of the jars is an explanation. Find everyone, and do as you please with it."

Art by Tempy Moore. 2nd great-granddaughter of Julia Temperance Adams DeLoach

Stunned, I went straight to that place she loved so much. There, in the warm sunlight, I wondered what I might find. Entering her little red-and-white garden shed, I found a shovel and then walked through the garden gate my father had built so many years ago. The whitewash came off on my hand as it always did. I found the spot where she once planted potatoes and began to dig. One by one, I unearthed the jars—

first one, then another, until ten lay on the ground in front of me. Each jar was light green, discolored to the point that you could not see inside. All were heavy except one. I figured that one must hold the letter, so I opened it.

Torn between sorrow and excitement, I sat in the middle of that small garden, and read the letter Mom had written with such care. In those clearly written lines, all was revealed: the story of the Confederate gold, the moonlight marriage, a midnight murder, and my ancestors' role in it all. She explained how she and my father saw it as a burden and didn't want to pass it on to us, choosing instead to teach us the value of hard work. She ended her letter by saying how proud she was of her children. "Keep your name good, pray often, and always try to do right."

An emotional mess, I began to cry. So many loved ones were gone, I felt alone, and no amount of gold could replace the loving family I missed. I thought about all the things money could buy and about all the trouble the contents of these jars had caused so many people over the years.

I remembered what my parents had taught me, that work is a blessing, while money and idleness can ruin lives. I thought about my ancestors and what they had been through. I knew what I had to do. Without looking inside any of the other jars, I reburied them—this time, deeper than before. I buried all but the one containing the letter. Lifting myself up off the ground, I brushed the dirt from my trousers. Jar in hand, I left the garden.

I placed that jar on a mantel to remind me of my family's rich history and my mother's enduring love. I decided that the true gold was the story Momma told–an intrinsically richer and far greater gift.

A jar of gold would surely glitter, I thought. But then, what did Shakespeare say? "All that glitters is not gold."

Little Joe's Success

Little Joe sat at his large mahogany desk, gazing out the window at the Atlantic Ocean. Sunlight danced across the water, and the warm sea breeze stirred the curtains. The sun shone bright, and the curtains swayed gently. He sipped his coffee, still steaming from the careful hands of Addie, the maid.

"I'm done! Yahoo," he shouted, loud enough for everyone to hear. "I'm always thrilled when I find out how one of my stories is going to end." He leaned back in his chair, a satisfied grin spreading across his face. Then, a fleeting thought struck him: Would the New Yorker be as thrilled as I am?

Addie appeared in the doorway, her expression a mix of curiosity and amusement.

"Can I help you, sir?"

"Yes, Addie, I want to dance!" Springing to his feet, he took Addie's soft, manicured, light chocolate-colored hand in his and began to lead her around the polished wooden floor, his voice bursting into song. *"I got sunshine on a cloudy day. When it's cold outside, I got the month of May."*

Taken by surprise, Addie raised her voice slightly, saying, "What is the matter with you?"

"I'm just plain happy, Addie. Just plain old happy." He replied, twirling her in a makeshift waltz. What did you put in my coffee anyway, to make me so happy?"

"I don't know what it was," she said, laughing as she pulled her hand free. "But I could sure use some, my own self," she said, smiling pensively.

"You'd better pour yourself a cup. Let's all have some breakfast around here. Where's my beautiful wife? I want a great big breakfast and the company of the people I love around me. It's a glorious day in Charleston, South Carolina!"

"Well, sir," Addie replied, a mischievous glint in her eye, "your wife might not want to have breakfast with you if she catches you dancing with me like a crazy man."

"Oh, Addie, I've been crazy for years. You can't expect me to change just because you're here? You're part of the family now. You're not the *help*. You're just here to help," he said, releasing her.

"I don't know if I can help you, as crazy as you are," she muttered, shaking her head as she walked away, a soft smile on her lips.

Just then, the phone rang. Little Joe answered it, saying, "City Morgue, you stab'em, we'll slab'em!"

"What the heck did you say?" laughed the voice on the other end.

"Would you prefer a simple hello?" All he heard on the other end was laughter.

"Never heard that one before," answered the caller.

"Is this you, Noah? I didn't look at the caller ID."

"Yes."

"Where are you at?"

"Aileen and I are in town, we just landed."

"Oh, great! Hurry over; we're about to have breakfast. You're just in time."

"We'll be there in a half an hour," Noah replied. "Gotta run- see you soon!"

Just as Little Joe hung up the phone, Diane entered the room.

"Great news, Di," he said, "The kids are here. They'll be over in thirty minutes. Let's get crackalackin' on the breakfast."

"That's wonderful! I'll tell Addie there will be company. If she is still here," Diane teased. "She says if you dance with her again, she's leaving."

"Oh, hell, she loves me. She couldn't live without us," he said laughingly.

"Hey! I finished my story for the New Yorker's Halloween edition!"

"Wonderful, what is it called?"

"Happy Hollowed Beings It's a new twist on scary stories. I think they'll love it."

"I'm sure they will," Diane said with a smile. "You can't seem to do anything wrong these days. Well, that is, except for your minor episodes of lunacy." She smiled.

Life had been good for them. They had built the house they'd always dreamed of in Charleston, their favorite city. A charming cultural hub steeped in history. With Joe's books selling well, they had the means to hire help, travel often, and indulge in simple pleasures.

One of their favorite pastimes was taking Joe's Boulevard motorcycle for long coastal rides. They loved visiting his cousin Donnie in North Myrtle Beach, where they'd enjoy a beer and make music. Don was a singer, like him, and a great guitar player.

Other times, they would ride south to historic Savannah. The city was founded by Masons from England. Released from debtor prisons, those Masons moved to the Americas, funded by the Grand Lodge of England. Most folks didn't know that, but he delved deep into its history and found it interesting.

"Anybody home?" came a voice from the front door. "Who lives in this beautiful house? Rockefeller?" Little Joe recognized his daughter's voice and ran to meet her.

"How are you? I've missed you both so much. How do you like the new house?"

"I love it so far," Aileen said. "Can't wait to see the rest of it!"

"Well, come on in, let me show you around."

Hearing the commotion, Diane came into the room and hugged them warmly.

"I told Addie you two were coming. She is whipping up a big breakfast. We can eat out on the patio overlooking the ocean–your dad just bought it for me."

"Wow! Now, he bought you an ocean. That's pretty nice of him," Noah said.

"Yep," Diane replied with a wink. "He says it's all mine. Says nothing's too good for me."

"That's right, Di," Joe said, slipping his arm around her, "Anything your little pea-picking heart desires. Now, let's head out to the patio and get comfortable. I'll get us a pot of coffee. Breakfast will be ready soon, and you know Addie's cooking is unbeatable."

The patio stretched the length of the house, offering a breathtaking view of the ocean. A section jutted out into the yard, surrounded by lush plants and trees that created a cozy, secluded haven. Below, the yard sloped gently toward the beach. Concrete framed a sparkling in-ground pool and hot tub, turning the space into a little slice of paradise.

As they settled in, Addie began bringing plates of food to the table.

"Let me help you, Addie," Diane offered, rising from her seat.

"I don't need help," Addie replied firmly. "You just sit yourself down and enjoy your family."

The smell was mouthwatering, and everyone was hungry. So Little Joe asked Noah to say a prayer before eating.

"Most Holy and Glorious Lord God, Thou great architect of Heaven and earth, who art the giver of all good gifts and graces, and who hast promised, that where there are two or more gathered in thy name, thou wilt be in the midst of them. In Thy name we assemble and meet together. Most humbly beseeching Thee to bless us in all our undertakings. That we might know and serve Thee aright. And that all our dealing might tend to thy glory and the salvation of our souls. Bless this family, Lord, bless this food, and thank you for all your blessings." And they all said, "So mote it be."

***

After breakfast, Diane led the couple to their room, suggesting they might want to freshen up a bit before the grand tour.

"We'll be out on the patio when you're unpacked and changed into something more comfortable. It's going to be a gorgeous day," she said. "Put your swimsuits on, if you like. Your dad always takes a swim after breakfast to work the calories off. He calls it his morning constitutional."

"That sounds like a great idea," Noah said, grinning.

An hour later, they joined Little Joe and Diane by the pool, laughter ringing out under the morning sun.

"That's a nice-looking bathing suit, Dad. Is it new?" Aileen asked, noticing the bright tropical pattern.

"Yes, it is. Just bought it. My last one was so old it had a hole in the knee."

"What, are you kidding me? I can never tell."

"Yes, I'm just kidding. Nothing around here is *that* old except the jokes."

The family swam for two hours before the sun grew too hot, forcing them to leave the pool to find some shade. They talked about all the things going on in their lives. Aileen graduated from Geneva College in Beaver Falls, PA, with a dual degree, running a successful online store selling custom-printed glasses and cups, teaching school and following in her father's footsteps as a writer. Noah had gone back to school to complete his master's. He was ready to open his own office, offering his services as a psychologist. They were all happy to hear so many positive things going on in each other's lives.

"I'm so hungry," Joe announced, rubbing his stomach. "I could eat the north end out of a southbound skunk. It's getting close to lunch. I'll have Addie make us up some sandwiches, and we can have drinks and eats under the shade of this big old oak tree. What do you say?"

Diane shook her head, laughing. "You never know what's going to come out of that man's mouth."

"Sounds good to me!" said Noah, laughing. "But I'll settle for a sandwich."

"Me too!" said Aileen.

On the patio, a large black metal table nestled beneath an ancient oak draped in Spanish moss. The shade, combined with the ocean breeze, created the perfect oasis for a midday meal. Addie soon appeared with a serving tray piled high with sandwiches arranged in a floral pattern, green leaf lettuce serving as the decorative leaves. Alongside were two pitchers of sweet tea- what Addie called "the wine of the South" – and a wicker basket brimming with fresh fruit.

"Addie, will you sit down and eat with us?" Little Joe asked warmly.

"No, I've got work to do in the kitchen," she replied, brushing off the offer with a smile. "Y'all go on and eat–I'm just fine."

After a short prayer offered by Little Joe, the family dug into the meal, their laughter and conversation carrying on the breeze.

Chapter 7

Good Therapy

The day passed quickly, and before long, night settled over them. Lying in bed, they listened to the waves splashing onto the beach. The warm night air drifted into the room, carrying the teasing scent of saltwater.

"It's nice here, isn't it, Noah?" Aileen said.

"It sure is. Your dad's books must be selling very well."

"He works late every night and is up early writing each morning," Mom said. "He has poured himself into his writing since his sister passed. I can't imagine the pain he must have felt, losing so many family members in such a short a time. They were so close, saw each other every day and went everywhere together. Their personalities and physical presence were so strong that it's hard for me to believe they are gone. I'm sure he misses them deeply. All his siblings are dead, except for Uncle Earl in Phoenix. He was really happy to see us today."

"I'd like to ask how he's really doing—give him a chance to open up if he wants to. I think I'll go to his study now and see if we can talk," Noah said.

"Always the counselor, aren't you?"

"I guess so. But everything is just too good around here. There must be something wrong. No one is this happy."

Noah enjoyed the coolness of the tile floor as his feet danced in the dark as he searched for his slippers. Wrapping a robe around him, he headed for his father-in-law's study. As he neared what Little Joe sometimes called his Sanctum Sanctorum, he heard muffled voices. Not wanting to disturb anyone, he waited a moment to hear if he recognized the voices. Turning to go back, he lost a slipper that refused to turn with him, causing him to grab the wall for support. A picture hanging there wobbled, making a loud noise as he tried to catch it.

"Who's there?" called a voice from within.

"Just me, sir. I was coming to see you and tripped over my own feet."

Opening the door, Joe laughed and bid him enter. "What's the matter, can't sleep?"

"No problem, just wanted to talk some more if it's okay with you," said Noah.

Entering the room, he found it empty except for the two of them. Curious as to what he had heard, he blurted out, "I thought I heard voices in here."

"You probably did. I talk to myself a lot these days. Used to think that was crazy, so I looked it up on the computer. It said people who talk to themselves are smarter. They're working through problems and finding solutions or something like that. I don't worry about it, one way or the other, anymore."

"What are you writing now, sir?"

"I'm not really; I'm thinking through possibilities. Brainstorming, if you will. You know, Noah, I'm glad you came by this evening. I have something I need to tell you. I think very highly of you, and, well, I love you like you're my own son. Can I trust you to keep a secret?"

"Yes, sir, you can trust me with your deepest, darkest secrets. After all, as a counselor, keeping secrets is kind of my business."

"Good! Because I have a whopper of a story to tell. It's going to take a good listener and a trusted confidant to handle it."

Joe launched into the entire story. He spoke of his great-great-grandfather, Tennessee Adams, and how the Confederate leaders, in disarray, absconded with the entire treasury. They left just before Richmond fell to the Union Army. He told of the disappearance of the Confederate treasure. He explained the Moonlight Marriage and Midnight Murder and how that knowledge both aided and tormented four generations of one family. Little Joe elaborated, "I think I know where that gold is."

When he was through, Noah took note of the grin on Joe's face and wondered if it was true, or if it was a story he was preparing to write. Dumbfounded, Noah rose from his armchair and looked intently at his father-in-law, and said, "That is the most amazing story I have ever heard, and I have heard some doozies. Is this a story for your next book? Or are you telling me that you're not a successful author, but a fabulously wealthy treasure hunter?"

"That depends. Can you process what I've told you–and accept the responsibility of carrying that knowledge?"

"Sir, maybe I should lie on the couch and let you counsel me–because honestly, I have no idea what to think. There is a lot to process there. I think I'd better sleep on it."

"Is my story, my secret, safe with you?"

"Yes, Sir, it is."

"Good, we will speak again tomorrow."

Noah left, both relaxed and confused. A little uncertain but sure there had to be a more logical answer to the story, he hoped the morning would bring a new and stronger understanding of their conversation.

The questions circling in his mind plagued him for an hour before the Sandman sprinkled his eyes with lovely dreams of gold.

Noah rose early enough to see the sun inch its way up over the ocean. It was a sight he never grew tired of. As he watched the giant orb come to life in all its glory, he tried to sort out the thoughts that raced through his head. Which parts were dreams, and which were unbelievably true? The only things he could count on were the brilliance of the sun, the beauty of the ocean, and his need for coffee.

Aileen arose, rested, and was anxious to meet the day. She found Noah sitting by the window, watching the ocean waves roll towards them and then slide back into the depths. She knew he was lost in thought.

"How did your talk with Father go last night?"

"Oh, very good, I think. He's a fascinating man."

"Did he tell you about his demons?"

"No demons, not yet. We will talk again today."

"Have you had coffee?"

"No, but I would dearly love some."

"I'll freshen up and go get us a cup."

As Noah sat contemplating the miracle of sunrise, he wondered if what Little Joe had told him could be true. He knew what his next question had to be. It was the one question that kept popping up in his mind over and over: "Why did his father-in-law say he thinks he knows where the gold is? Why the uncertainty? If he doesn't know where it is, how did he buy all these things?" Noah realized he was squinting in thought and made himself quit. "The truth will come out," he murmured. "Today might be the most important day of my life. I think I had better say a special prayer. Dear Lord, in all my dealings, may I do only those things that honor Christ."

When Aileen returned with the coffee, she opened the door to find Noah still gazing out the window. Down the hall, he heard his father-in-law saying loudly, "Addie's going to cook up a mess of hot cakes and sausage if you're hungry." Then, more quietly, he added, "It's great to have people in the house—not just me and the spirits."

"What did he mean by that, I wonder, Aileen?"

"Who knows?" she responded. "I know you're hungry. Better get ready for some more good cooking."

After breakfast, they took another swim in the large kidney-shaped pool; then Diane asked Aileen to go to town with her. She needed a few things and wanted to show off one of her favorite stores. Aileen agreed, and after changing, they left. Noah saw this as the perfect time to talk again with Little Joe.

"Sir, I have some questions. Can we talk out here on the patio?"

"Sure. Did you think about what I told you?"

"Yes, I have. I'm wondering why you were uncertain as to the whereabouts of the" he looked around and whispered, "*gold?*"

"Ha, ha, ha,' Little Joe laughed. Funny how just the word itself brings about a change in all of us. Tell me something. If you had access to loads of money, what would you do with it?"

"Well, I'd like to travel—there's so much I want to see."

"Would you finish getting your degree so you could open your own office and practice counseling?" Little Joe asked.

"Yes, definitely!" Noah answered, "I wouldn't want it to drastically change our lives–just enhance our security and help us grow culturally. I truly believe that our happiness in this life comes from the one who holds the key to the next. *Gold would be nice. But God is essential.*"

"In that case, Noah, I know exactly where I think the gold is because I buried it myself. The reason I say 'I think' is because I never really gazed upon it. It was in mason jars that were discolored from the earth. I didn't ever want to have to say I saw it, so I didn't look inside. I'm also not sure what the law is concerning this stash. I just knew I had to tell someone before I was gone, and the treasure would be lost forever. I felt certain I could share my secret with you. And it is a great relief to have done so. I will tell you where it is. You'll probably marvel at how many times you stepped right over it, never knowing."

"Sir, I have another question for you."

"Not to be intrusive or impertinent, but if you have never touched that gold, how did you obtain such amazing success in so short a time?"

"I believe the gold helped me psychologically–but not financially. Knowing it was there made a great difference in my attitude and optimism. I could better focus on my work. I almost turned to it, but something pushed me to look inward and use the talent God gave me."

"You say you were induced? Who encouraged you? Your wife?"

"Yes, of course, she was an inspiration and a great help. Besides her, I sought out the wisest counselors I could find, and I put the problem in their hands."

"I discovered the laws of nature. That thoughts are not a lot of fleeting nothings, but very real objects that must be governed. That knowledge gave me the ability to turn desire into gold. It is a law of nature that one can change the thought process of desire into its financial sameness. If one has desire and mixes it with faith, it gives life, command, and animation to the impulse of thought. I learned how to use faith to heal my most serious maladies. Faith is the foundation of all miracles and all things mysterious that science cannot understand. Faith mixed with prayer gives you direct contact with the infinite. Faith turns ordinary vibes of thoughts into a holy state. When you hear that faith can move mountains, you should take it literally. Faith is the only known cure for disastrous outcomes. I have learned that faith can be harnessed and used in practical ways. And that, Noah, is my secret."

"I understand some of what you're saying–but I'd like to know more. But wait, you said counselors. Care to elaborate?"

Little Joe cut the conversation short, saying, "No, I don't! Not now, anyway. Maybe later."

Just as Noah thought he was getting his father-in-law to open up, the phone rang, and it was Diane. She wanted to take Aileen sightseeing up the coast. She thought they might spend the night in a hotel in Myrtle. Noah and Little Joe talked about it and decided to let them go alone, while they stayed and enjoyed some male bonding.

"Keep in touch with us; let us know where you stay," said Joe.

"Noah," he said, "I want to show you my Sanctum Sanctorum–like you've never seen it before."

"Sure, did I miss something?"

"I think you might find it interesting to know how it was built."

Entering his office, Joe held the door for Noah, allowing him to step in first before closing it firmly behind them.

"This door is solid wood–three inches thick–with an R-value of 1.86. It's cut to fit perfectly, top and bottom, with insulation strips all around. I wanted to make this room as quiet as possible. The inside and outside walls are insulated with blown cellulose insulation three and five-eighths inches thick, for an R-factor of almost R-13. The solid wood paneling in the hallway adds another R-0.32. There is a half-inch of drywall that contributes 0.56. That is covered with a quarter-inch of foam on the inside for an additional R-value of 1.32. Then a quarter-inch of paneling on top of that provides 0.31. If you total up all the R-values, the U-factor comes to about U-15.51. The sound-deadening properties are remarkable. Still, I could hear you bouncing off the walls the other night, and you could hear me a little. But still, the soundproofing here is excellent.

When I'm working, I need quiet. Even more so, when I am in search of ideas."

Joe gestured toward the single, large window on the wall. "The window is a bit of a weak point for soundproofing, but I solved that. I crafted a foam insert two inches thick, covered it with vinyl wall covering that matched the walls, and added handles to make it easy to place snugly inside the window opening. It seals out all light and sound. Sit in that armchair, and I'll show you what it's like when I meditate here." He gestured behind his desk. "I had some buttons installed. One will turn on the DVD player. The music is *Wholetones* by Michael Tyrrell. This music can transport us spiritually—and transform us physically. He has created beautiful sounds in seven healing frequencies. These are frequencies that were locked away for more than three thousand years. We identify frequencies using a unit of measurement called the hertz. Hertz measures sound as one vibration cycle per second. In ancient times, at least seven of these frequencies were used to heal and protect."

"This CD includes seven of those frequencies, each captured in a song—it's one of the most miraculous listening experiences you'll ever have. I got my copy as a gift from a dear friend—Pastor Cynthia Antinossi, who owned WXED 107.3 FM. I love the way it helps me to meditate. It takes me to an entirely different place."

Joe pressed another button, dimming the room lights. "This button controls the lights. I can have complete darkness or switch to black light. With the foam covering the window and the soundproofing in place, I can create an environment free of distractions. It's designed to help me meditate, explore the subconscious mind, and tap into infinite intelligence."

"As a counselor, you know the mind is a mysterious and wonderful world. Napoleon Hill said, "Anything the mind of man can conceive and believe, he can achieve." I'm acting on that belief. I have seen things with my mind and done things that are amazing, even to me. I could not begin to explain them. For me, exploring the mind has become a beautiful, ever-deepening journey. That is only possible when one allows positive thoughts to dominate his thinking. It's when one allows negative thoughts to enter that ugly, evil things happen. In that respect, we are all the master of our ship and our fate. I seek wisdom, not knowledge. Create the right environment, and you can tap into the subconscious mind. Wisdom thrives in secret shades and quiet spaces designed for contemplation, there to deliver her sacred oracles. And there I'll be to greet her."

Noah, listening intently to the music and Joe's words, adjusted himself in his chair, saying, "This is truly an amazing feeling. I understand you fully. I wish I had a room like this."

Joe smiled. "Some time ago, I read how Napoleon Hill utilized an invisible council. I tried to do the same. I chose my heroes to counsel me, men I wanted to emulate, like George Washington, Ben Franklin and Abraham Lincoln. I added Jesus and John the Baptist. I studied each man so I could understand their essence. I imagined regular meetings with them. Of course, I knew they were imaginary–but over time, they took on distinct personalities. George was always the gentleman. Ben was a jokester who loved to push everyone's buttons. Jesus was calming and serene, and John was fiery and forceful. I continued those meetings for years–and eventually, others joined in."

"One day, I was flying at thirty-eight thousand feet when I looked out the window and saw something. It was a sunny day with white, puffy cirrocumulus clouds in abundance. It was not long after my mother had passed away. There, sitting on the whitest cloud, was my mom. She wore an ankle-length dress with a white button-up top, her bare feet swinging like a carefree eighteen-years-old. She had a huge smile on her face and was kicking her feet like a young girl on a swing, without a care in the world. She looked straight at me and, without moving her lips, said, "You know what you have to do," she said. "You know what you said you would do, remember?""

"Tears filled my eyes as I soaked in the amazing sensation of having her back again. I knew she wasn't real, but I didn't care. I didn't want it to end–but after several minutes, I let it go. When she was gone, I reached inside the pocket on the back of the seat in front of me and pulled out the barf bag. With pen in hand, I began to write a poem about my experience with cancer. In twenty minutes, I was done, and the phraseology struck me as very good. I could not believe I was able to write something so good in just twenty minutes. My visions of her started coming more frequently. The more I saw her, the better my writing seemed to become. Another poem poured out of me, then a family story."

Noah interrupted, "What did she mean when she said, 'You know what you have to do?'"

Joe took a deep breath. "When I was young, my father was my hero. His loss was traumatic for me. Afterward, I promised myself that I would build a monument to him someday. It was a silly idea for a child of only sixteen. I planned it all, studied the area where it would go, and kept the plan alive in my mind. Since I loved my whole family, I decided to make it large enough to include them all. But I never acted on the plan. When I began writing, I did so for the enjoyment. I had always been drawn to it. While I had been told I had some talent in the area, my writing was never for others to see, just myself, and for the mental therapy and the enjoyment of it. One day, after reading one of my stories at a guild meeting, I had the idea of putting all my personal stories together in an episodic memoir. Suddenly, a light came on and I knew what she wanted me to do! Through my writings, I could immortalize my family members. Celebrate them within its pages and not with concrete. I finally realized what she meant—she didn't want me to use the gold. She wanted me to mine the gold buried deep in my mind—and write the story of our lives together."

"Wow, that is one heck of a story. I thought yesterday was good. But this! This is a story that must be written," Noah said.

"Do you think I'm crazy, Noah? Do I have something to worry about?"

Noah laughed. "Crazy! I don't think you're crazy, well, no crazier than me anyway. You've developed a unique coping mechanism through your imagination. You use it to process things from your past. Things you may not have fully faced yet–and it'll likely continue helping you in the future. You've built a support group from your memories, research, and understanding of others. That's a work of genius! As for having anything to worry about, your group seems to be made up of fine, upstanding people. Now, if your group included Hitler, Mussolini, Stalin–and later adding Saddam Hussein and Osama bin Laden–then we would have something to worry about."

"I don't think so, sir, as long as you have it under control. It looks to me like you have used your imagination to great advantage and had a lot of fun doing it."

"So, is that why you never delved into the gold? You were following the dictates of your mom and your invisible council? Is that right, sir?"

"Pretty much. I wanted to see if I could do it on my own, and I did. Hard work and using parts of the brain that seldom get used."

"I appreciate you telling me all of this. I know it's not easy for you. I want you to know that I will never tell a soul. Sharing this with me should make your life easier. It's not good to keep things bottled up inside you. Did you ever tell your wife?"

"No, I have never told anyone until today, and it sure is good to tell someone. I feel a little lighter, more peaceful. Thanks, Noah, for being the trusted friend I thought you would be and allowing me to share my story."

Chapter 8

The Unexpected Guest

As the South Carolina sun reached its peak over Charleston, Noah and Little Joe basked in its warmth, sipping iced tea by the pool. Diane and Aileen would be spending one more day on their sightseeing trip, promising to be home sometime after sunset.

"Noah, I usually don't drink when I'm working, but since you're here–and I'm not writing–I think I'd like to have a beer. You want one?"

"Sure, sounds good. I'm on vacation."

"It's Friday, why don't I ask Addie to whip us up some sandwiches and send her home early so she can enjoy her family? We won't need her for anything. We can eat leftovers for dinner or head into town."

"Fine with me," answered Noah, rubbing more suntan lotion on his face and arms.

After lunch, Noah asked Little Joe about the gold. He grew more curious, but would not directly ask where it was. He knew Joe would not tell until he was ready.

Little Joe sensed his interest and told him he wanted Aileen to be there when he revealed his secret, saying it wouldn't be right to tell one and not the other. There was his daughter, Amber, who must be told as well. She was living and working in Hollywood, California. He wanted everyone to be on the same page and more or less in agreement on how to handle it. It was the one thing that worried him most.

The afternoon passed quickly as they discussed Wholetones music. Little Joe tried to explain the soothing sounds of Wholetones. He was excited about its healing powers and his ability to think creatively while listening to the compositions.

"I've read that in ancient times, music was used for its therapeutic value. In ancient Greece, physicians used flutes, lyres, and zithers for healing. Vibration was used to aid in digestion and to treat psychological instabilities. Aristotle wrote that flute music could stimulate strong emotions and cleanse one's soul. Ancient Egyptians described musical incantations for healing. The curative power of music has been well-documented, but these new high frequencies are geared exclusively for that purpose. Not only can they heal, they can lift one to a higher plane of thought level few ever achieve. And I'm pretty sure Wholetones has cornered the market. I love it!"

Later that day, Little Joe and Noah drove into town for fresh oysters at Hyman's on 215 Meeting Street– one of Little Joe's favorite places in downtown Charleston. A near collision with another vehicle spurred Little Joe to say, "You'd better keep me alive, Noah, if you ever want to find out where that gold is."

"I'm trying," Noah laughed.

As darkness fell over the city, it seemed to come alive with people enjoying the nightlife and tourists walking the streets, admiring its historic architecture and homes with brightly colored doors. Walking back to their car and all the way home, Little Joe told Noah interesting tidbits he had learned about Charleston's history. Back home, Little Joe suggested they play his Wholetones CD and meditate under the black light in his office.

"Once you start exploring the inner mind, it becomes habit-forming. The gentle moments of pure power become so enjoyable, simple, and easy that you hate to stop. It's energizing and clarifying, a sensation like no other. You will gladly give up all negative thoughts and influences in exchange for a higher consciousness. It's my end-of-the-day gift to myself. In exchange for that time, I'm given hope and faith in abundance, along with rare insights into problems and often solutions. You gain personal satisfaction and a sense of completeness—mentally, physically, and spiritually."

Noah was anxious to re-examine the place that spurred Little Joe's creativity to new heights.

As Little Joe took his chair behind the great desk, Noah closed the door behind him and took a seat to the left of the door, so they faced each other. Little Joe clicked a button that caused a stereophonic sound to instantly fill the room.

Just as he did, he thought he heard a crash outside. He paused for a few seconds, assumed it was his imagination, and went back to what he was doing. Adjusting the sound down to more of a background level, he again heard noise.

"Did you hear that, Noah?"

"Yes."

Just then, the door opened, and a stocky man of average height rushed in. In his hand was a revolver pointed squarely at Little Joe.

"Who are you, and what do you want?" Little Joe said with a slightly raised voice.

"I'm your worst nightmare!" the man replied.

"You're mistaken—I don't have nightmares. I don't accept them."

"Well then, I'll be your first!"

"I don't know who you are, but you don't need that gun in this house. It won't serve you here!" Little Joe said.

"I'll hang on to it anyhow, if it's all the same to you," the man barked back.

"Tell us what you want. How can we help you?"

"My name is Michael Bon. My great-great-grandfather was Jack Bon. Does that name ring a bell?"

Little Joe sat silent, listening to every word.

"He was shot to death in 1898. Murdered over a little thing like gold. Does anything come to mind? My father and his father lived in Johnson City, near Tiner's Hill, all their lives.

They worked there and kept watch on your kin. Waited for any sign of that missing gold to show up. They were certain your family was responsible for Jack Bon's murder. They knew your family had that gold! But there was never any sign of it. It was me who finally figured out that it wasn't there any longer. I was the one smart enough to know that it had moved from Tennessee to Pennsylvania, and now maybe Charleston, huh? I will not wait like my father and his did. I want that gold, and I'm going to get it. I'll have it—or you'll die."

"Like I said before, fear does not reside here, so that gun will not serve you, and I will not let you harm anybody. Put the gun down, and I will tell you what you want to know."

"I am not fooling around. You will do as I say, or you're a dead man."

"I'm not afraid of dying. I've made my peace with the King of Kings. But what would you gain if I were dead? Nothing! You need me alive, and I need you to put that gun down; then I'll tell you what you want. Rest assured, no one here will try to harm you. We will not call the police now or later. You can have what you want, but only after I am sure my family is safe."

"Tell me where the gold is, and I will go."

"You're not being rational; you have not thought this through, have you? How will you get that much gold home? How will you explain your newfound wealth to your friends and neighbors? How will you convert it to cash to begin with? It is very old you know. It has numismatic value, not just the spot market conversion rate value. Anyone who sees it will know that it is old. They will be suspicious, there will be talk, and before long, you will be telling the police everything, and I will be implicated. Put the damn gun down and let's work out a plan that'll work for you."

"None of your tricks. I want the gold now!"

"Sir, maybe you should tell him before someone gets hurt," Noah said.

"Happy to, just as soon as he lays down that gun, Noah. He's unstable. If I tell him what he wants to know, he may shoot us anyhow. Our wives may return any time. I can't have this crazy man waving a pistol around when they do."

Little Joe displayed only calm as he sat behind his desk in his leather armchair. He hadn't covered the large window behind him with the usual foam, and he knew the lights of a car would be seen coming up the driveway if, indeed, Diane were to come home. He hoped she wouldn't. He had left the Wholetones playing softly in the background, and the lights were turned on.

He worried the man had brought with him such hatred that he could not be calmed. A man who cannot be calmed is a very dangerous man indeed.

When Little Joe caught a glimpse of light coming through the window, he knew he had to be concerned for the lives of his wife and daughter. The game had changed; he had to do something now.

"Mr. Bon, will you please put the gun down so we can talk? I offer you my hand in friendship, and I promise you gold," Little Joe said quietly, rising from his chair.

"Sit down! Sit down! No tricks!"

Little Joe knew instinctively that the man would not go peacefully, and he would have to initiate force.

With his right hand, he flipped off the lights, plunging the room into near-total darkness. Suddenly, there arose a loud thunderous explosion from Bon's gun, answered by two more from the 9mm Little Joe kept hidden under his row of buttons.

Noah stood motionless. In the flash of light from the guns, he saw Little Joe take a bullet to the chest and fall over his desk.

Bon stood frozen, stunned—as if he didn't realize he'd been shot and should fall.

Noah flew into a rage, seeing Little Joe murdered. He remembered how he took down running backs in his days on the gridiron at Geneva College. He swept forward like a storm, taking Bon down like a defensive linebacker. He tackled Bon hard, driving him across the room, crashing onto the floor and causing the gun to pop out of the man's hands, just like the football fumbles he used to cause in college—except this was no game. Once he had the man, he could not resist giving him a pounding. He wanted to pound the sense into him that his father-in-law had tried so hard verbally to do. Bon didn't respond–two 9mm rounds to the chest had ended his treasure-hunting days for good.

Screams erupted from the hallway.

"Oh my God, what happened?" exclaimed Aileen.

Diane and Aileen had been coming down the hall when they heard the gunshots. They opened the door, adding light to the room and exposing the bullet wounds in Bon. Diane immediately ran to Little Joe, who lay motionless, bent over that great desk.

"That bastard killed your father! Little Joe's dead!" Noah cried out.

***

Noah pulled out his phone and stepped into the hallway, dialing 911.

Before long, the room was full of policemen, crime scene investigators, and paramedics. One detective asked Diane and Aileen to wait in another room. Another was questioning Noah, who told him it was an armed robbery that had gone horribly wrong.

"The man was crazy!" Noah said. "We couldn't talk to him. He was waving that gun around, dead-set on hurting someone, so my father-in-law shot him. It was dark and Little Joe must've had a gun hidden under his desk. None of us knew the man."

Across the room, the paramedic examining the body called out to his partner, "I have a pulse! Get that gurney over here; we need to transport this man to Roper Hospital fast."

The police determined they had enough to file an initial report. They let the family follow the ambulance, but warned them not to leave town.

At Roper Hospital, Little Joe's gurney was wheeled into the emergency room, where a doctor and a team of nurses were waiting to examine him. Removing his clothes, they found a Masonic Past Master's medallion in his jacket pocket. The bullet had struck the medallion, deflected, and went into his chest just a short distance, entering not far but very close to the heart. Just like his great-great-grandfather, Tennessee Adams, a medallion had saved his life.

Further examination found he had struck his temple on a large paperweight that lay on his desk. A nurse cleaned the wound and stopped the bleeding. An X-ray technician captured images to pinpoint where the bullet had lodged. Others prepared the patient for an operation. The bullet had to be removed soon.

Two hours later, the doctor walked into the waiting room to console Little Joe's family. "

"He's going to be okay," he said.

They sighed with relief— 'Oh, thank God,'—and tears of joy followed.

"He may have some pain for a while, but we can manage that. The surgery went well. I removed a bullet from very near his heart, but there was no serious damage." He proceeded to tell them how the medallion had saved his life. "He's a very lucky man!" he said, handing them the medallion, dented at the edge. "I have never seen anything like it."

Noah replied, "I'm not sure if it was luck or the Almighty. He doesn't believe in luck. He must have a guardian angel because something like this would never happen again in a hundred years."

"Actually, it's happened in his family twice–in 151 years," Noah mumbled, marveling at the odds.

"What do you mean?" asked the doctor.

"Never mind, Doc. Just thinking out loud. Thank you, sir, for patching him up," Noah said.

"Can we go in and see him?" Diane asked.

"Yes, but only for a moment–he needs rest. Also, there was a gash on his left temple. I stitched it up, but he'll definitely have a pounding headache."

After an emotional visit with Little Joe, the three of them readied to leave the hospital for home. On the way out, they ran into the police detective who stopped in to see how he was doing. "How's your husband?" he asked Diane.

"He's doing fine," she said. "He will be okay, according to the doctor."

"I'm very happy for you all," replied the officer. "I have some information on the suspect for you. He is Michael Bon from Johnson City, Tennessee. We don't know why he was in Charleston–or why he targeted your home. Have any of you ever heard of him before? Can you think of any reason he would want to harm you?"

"No, I didn't know him, and Little Joe didn't know him either. He seemed to be crazy!" Noah answered.

"It's a little strange, but we will keep the investigation open for a while. Maybe we will discover more answers."

"Did he have any family?" asked Noah.

"He had a wife, we think. We won't know much for sure until we get information back from Johnson City P.D., tomorrow."

"Please keep us informed, officer. We would like to know the reasons behind this ourselves," Aileen said.

On returning home, the police had removed the body and were just finishing up their crime scene investigation, placing tape that read 'POLICE LINE, DO NOT CROSS' across the door that led to Little Joe's office.

"I can't believe this!" Diane said. "How could something like this happen to us?"

"We are so blessed that Little Joe will be coming home, and he will be okay," Noah said. "It could have been so much worse."

"It's not the same without Dad in the house," said Aileen. "Nothing will ever be the same again."

"That's not so," Noah countered. "Little Joe will be coming home, and he is going to be writing, and everything will get back to normal. We can't let this destroy us. We can't let it change who we are. Little Joe would not want that to happen. He would be the first one to say, "We have to get past all this negativity.""

"Hope you're right," Aileen answered.

Diane had shown strength up to this point, but now, when she was forced to face a night alone without Little Joe, she realized how close she had come to losing him. Her legs became weak, and the horrible truth of all that had happened came rushing out of her in tears. Noah took her into his massive arms, held her close, and allowed all the anger and pain to rush out of her while in a safe place.

"Let it out, ma'am—you've earned it."

The next day, they were all up at sunrise, showered, dressed, and ready to go. Breakfast would take time they didn't want to waste, so they made peanut butter toast, filled a to-go cup with Paul Newman's Own dark, rich coffee from the Keurig coffee maker, grabbed the newspaper from the porch, and headed for the hospital.

Traffic was light that early Saturday morning. Noah took the wheel while Aileen read the paper aloud. The headline read, "Burglar shot to death by local author."

"Oh my God, it made the front page!" Aileen exclaimed. "Everyone's going to be talking about this."

"I'm afraid it's not going to go away anytime soon. The papers will blow it up, and they will be after us for comments. We had better be prepared." Noah said.

"You're right, Noah. They will probably be waiting for us at the hospital. Turn right onto Courtenay Drive and go around to the back. I'm not ready for the newspaper people yet," said Diane.

Inside, they slipped past the reporters and made their way to Little Joe's critical care room. Once there, they met the detective on the case.

"Good morning, Sir," Noah said. "Have you learned any more about that guy?"

"No, not yet. But there's another issue–the doctor's examining your father-in-law now. It seems he has no memory of the other night. The doctor thinks it could be temporary–either from shock or the blow to his head. I was hoping to get a statement from him, but it will have to wait. I have to run now, but I'll be back later to check on him. If you recall anything, give me a call–the number's on the card I left last night."

Noah and the girls were still trying to process his words and said nothing as he walked away.

"I hope he doesn't stay like that," Aileen said. "That's scary."

Diane opened the door to her husband's room and found the doctor shining a light into Little Joe's eyes and looking intently.

"Look up at the ceiling. Now look down. Look to your right. Now your left. I don't see anything out of the ordinary, but we'd better have you examined by a neurologist."

Turning to leave, the doctor saw Diane at the door.

"You must be the wife?"

"Yes, doctor, I'm Diane. How is he doing?"

"Your husband is coming along nicely. However, he is suffering from headaches, and we discovered this morning that he does not have full use of his memory. It could be shock–or something more serious. We just don't know right now. We will have to keep him another day or so and have a neurologist examine him. We have to make sure that when he is released, he can take care of himself. Don't worry–the surgery went very well. We're expecting a full recovery on that front. He will be sitting up by the end of the day and walking soon. But this memory thing is something else. If you are asking me how bad it is? This we will have to determine."

"Doctor, have you ever seen this happen before?"

"Yes, many times. But it usually doesn't last long. We will just have to watch and see."

"Thank you, Doctor. Can we visit with him now? Does he know who we are?"

"Mr. McKirdy, you have company. Do you recognize these two with me?"

"Yes, that's my wife. How are you, honey?" Little Joe said.

"I'm fine, dear, Diane said with tears streaming down her face. "Do you know these two with me?"

"Yes. Hi Aileen, hi Noah."

"God, I'm glad you know who we are," said Diane, wiping her eyes with a coffee napkin.

"I'll give you all some time. I've got rounds to make," the doctor said.

"Thank you, Doctor," they all said.

"You're having some trouble remembering things, it seems," Diane said.

"Yes, some things are a little cloudy. I have a terrible headache."

"You're going to be okay, darling. Don't worry about anything. Just get well."

"Hi, Sir," Noah said. "I'm so glad to see you doing so well. I was really worried about you. It is such a relief to hear your voice. You will never know."

"Good to see you all. I can't wait to go home," Little Joe said.

"Won't be long, Dad," Aileen said.

"I brought you some writing paper and a pen so you can take notes and write down any thoughts you have. We want you well again."

"Thank you, honey. You're always so thoughtful. Thank you all for coming."

Little Joe's nurse came in to check his vitals. When she was satisfied everything was normal, she told the family, "I'm Darlene Thomason–your husband's nurse. Take a few more minutes, if you like, but my patient is going to need to rest. We don't want to overdo it. You can come back at noon. Visiting hours are on the wall in the hallway. I have your telephone number. If anything changes, I'll call you right away. If you have any questions, feel free to call. I'll give you a code number. You will need that to get any information over the phone."

"Thanks, Darlene. Honey, we will be leaving now. If you need anything at all, just call me. We will be back later. Get some rest."

Still groggy from the medication, Joe whispered, "Bye-bye."

Chapter 9

Damage Control

As the only one who knew Little Joe's secret, Noah felt isolated and burdened. Since Little Joe was in no condition to do anything, Noah felt it was up to him to protect the family and their interests. He needed to remember everything and make sense of it all. He wondered if Bon had a son or wife who knew where he was going, someone who might have followed him, anyone who could possibly show up at the house waving another gun. He imagined all the things that could go wrong and wanted to be prepared. Or, had Bon kept his plans secret even from those closest to him? Noah resolved to examine every possibility and eliminate any threat. Little Joe would not be any help. Noah decided to travel to Johnson City on his own and see what he could learn. As he ran the likelihoods through his mind, he thought about what Little Joe had told him about the gold, how it could be as much of a torment as a blessing. He was beginning to understand.

The first problem he would face was whether to tell Aileen Little Joe's secret. He wanted desperately to share the burden with someone who could help him think things through. But it was not his place to tell, and Little Joe was no longer capable. The questions weighed heavily on his mind. His immediate problem was how to explain the need to rent a car and drive to Johnson City.

*****

Sunday found Little Joe better in many ways. He could sit up, but was not yet able to walk because of the lifeline tentacles that kept watch over his vitals: his heart monitor wires, the intravenous tube in his wrist, and his oxygen level monitor. These were items that were just there to help him, but they made his condition look worse than it was. He was healing nicely, and his vitals were normal, so they moved him from the Critical Care Unit into a private room. Diane was relieved to spend more unrestricted time with him. However, he would not be able to go home until a specialist evaluated his memory problems. Everyone prayed he would regain that function soon.

The three of them left early to visit Little Joe. Aileen and Noah left midmorning to do some shopping, leaving Diane alone in his hospital room. She was peppering him with questions when a new doctor entered. He was a stocky-built man, dressed in khakis, a light green shirt, and a tie, and wearing a white doctor's smock.

"Good morning, Mr. McKirdy. I'm Doctor Brian Fredrick, your neurologist. I'm told you're having trouble remembering things. Can you tell me about that?" Drawing up a chair, the doctor sat next to Little Joe's bed. With a notebook in his lap, he crossed one leg over the other.

"Well, I can remember a lot of things, but other stuff seems cloudy. I just don't have any recollection at all, really."

"Dr. Guffey's report says you were shot at close range and had a pretty bad bump on the left temple area of your head. Did you notice any memory problems before that time?"

"No," replied Little Joe. "I don't remember having any problems, and that shooting, well, I don't remember any of that!"

Diane interjected, "His mind has always been sharp. He never had any trouble before."

"Mrs. McKirdy, how is his memory, other than the events of that night? Does he seem to know everyone?"

"Yes, he knows the family and even mentioned friends of ours. He seems fine except for that event."

"Mr. McKirdy, I'm going to perform a few tests to try and determine what type of help you need," said the doctor. He checked Little Joe's reflexes, sensory function, balance, and other physiological aspects of his brain, including the nervous system. He asked him questions to test his judgment, questions about general information, and historical events. The doctor asked him about current events, like who was the President.

"I think we can rule out Alzheimer's and other forms of dementia. I would like to have some imaging tests performed, an MRI and a CT scan to look for damage or abnormalities. We want to rule out tumors. We'll need to do blood tests in case there is an infection or nutritional deficiency."

"Can I go home today, Doc?" Little Joe asked.

"I don't think we can get it all done that fast. You may have to stay with us another day or so," the doctor said.

"At least we are getting to the bottom of things," Diane said.

***

Monday morning brought no relief for Noah, who had the same old questions flooding his brain. He was uncertain as to whether he should keep Little Joe's secret. Being the sole keeper of the story was becoming a heavy burden.

Aileen woke to a distant Noah sitting in his favorite chair, the one with the spectacular view of the ocean. There, he watched the sun rise each morning.

"Is it up yet, Hon?"

"It's just getting good. But there is no bad time to watch. I never tire of it."

"You sound kind of detached; you're thinking of Dad, aren't you?" Aileen questioned.

"Yes, I'm doing some soul-searching, some self-analysis."

"What is it?" she said.

"That detective asked if I knew anything about that guy, and I said no. I really don't know anything for certain. I know what I was told, but I'm sworn to secrecy. I don't know if I can keep this secret any longer. Don't know what to do."

"Did my dad ask you to keep a secret?" asked Aileen.

"Yes," Noah replied, "and the worst part is, he doesn't remember what he told me or even that he told me. I'm the keeper of a secret that has no point."

"Maybe you should tell me," Aileen said.

"He wanted to tell you himself. That was important to him. How can I violate that trust? Yet, if I don't speak up, there may be consequences." Noah said.

"What kind of consequences? Is it something we *need* to know?" Aileen asked.

"I don't know! I just don't know! I think I need to take a little trip. Maybe that will answer my questions. Do you trust me, Aileen?"

"Of course, I trust you, but if you know something, we'd better deal with it together," she said.

"I'm going to rent a car today and do some investigating of my own. When I get back, I will know what to do," Noah said.

"Where are you going?" she asked.

"Johnson City, Tennessee."

"Noah, that's where that man was from! Why do you want to go there?"

"I need to know if he has any partners we might expect a visit from."

"I'll go with you!" Aileen said.

"No, your mother and father need you here. I'm going to rent a car and drive there. I checked it out on MapQuest, and it's almost a five-hour drive. If I leave soon, I can be there around noon. I'll check with the police there, the courthouse, and the library. See what their newspapers are saying." Noah said.

"How long will you be gone? I don't want you to leave us."

"It shouldn't take me long," said Noah. "I'll call you when I get there and tell you what I've learned. If I can, I will just stay overnight and come back tomorrow."

Noah knew if Bon had family, they might know his reasons for being in Charleston. If he had cohorts, or if there were more crazies in the family, maybe they would be getting another visit. And, perhaps the next time, his wife or his mother–in–law would be injured. He had to make sure that didn't happen.

"I want you to call me and keep me up to date. Please be careful!" said Aileen.

Noah packed an overnight bag and had coffee while he waited for the car rental company to show up with a black Ford Focus. He thought it best to be as inconspicuous as possible while playing detective.

Diane came into the kitchen just as Noah was pulling out of the driveway. Aileen explained that he had work-related business to take care of. Diane thought it odd, but was more focused on seeing Little Joe and hoping he improved.

Merging onto I-26 West, Noah settled in for the 265-mile drive to the Tennessee line, followed by another fifteen miles to Johnson City. With hours on the road ahead of him, his mind churned.

In football, he always knew the person he was matched up against. In this game, he didn't. The smart move was to find out if there were any other players involved. He couldn't leave it to the police; by the time they figured things out, it could be too late.

Had he moved quickly enough? Was his family safe? Or had he left them in danger, with someone already in Charleston, ready to strike? The more he thought about it, the more he worried. Picking up his cell phone, he called Aileen.

"Hi, what are you doing?"

"I'm with Mom at the hospital, getting a cup of coffee. What is it?"

"I don't want to alarm you, because I'm sure there is no reason to, but why don't you and your mom stay downtown in a hotel tonight? That way, you can have a nice dinner out and be close to the hospital. I would feel better if you were not at the house alone."

"You're starting to scare me!" Aileen said.

"I'm just overthinking, no real reason. What do you say? You stay downtown tonight, and I'll be home tomorrow."

"Okay, I'll run home and get a few things for us, and surprise Mom later with a room key. Might be fun!" Aileen said.

"Good! I'm driving, so talk to you later, okay?"

"Okay, bye for now."

Noah felt better knowing the ladies would be safe. The sun was rising behind him as he headed northwest. Between traffic and checking his fuel level, he contemplated how to conduct his investigation. The local newspaper would have stories on it, no doubt. They might have family members listed. He could get a newspaper from the library. The courthouse would have census or tax data that he could bring up. The address would be easy to locate. What would he find? There was no way of knowing. But one thing was certain in Noah's mind: the best defense was a good offense.

The Investigation

Noah arrived in Johnson City at twelve-thirty in the afternoon. Tired and sore from driving, he went straight to the Holiday Inn. Too exhausted to think of his strategy, all he wanted was a shower and coffee.

After checking in, he grabbed a coffee from near the front desk and went to his room. Once there, he opened his computer and Googled the addresses for the police station and library. He learned the Johnson City library was on 100 W Millard Street. They would have the latest newspapers. He wanted to read them before going to the police station on 601

East Main Street. Since they were very near one another, it would make it easier for him.

He lay across his bed on his back after finishing his coffee and rested. His mind rehashed all he had experienced and his reason for being there. Slowly, he gathered himself for the task, raising himself from the bed that was so welcoming. After showering, he felt more like continuing his mission.

The Johnson City Public Library was the most beautiful library Noah had ever seen. He looked up at the large clock above the counter. It was just one-thirty; there was plenty of time.

"Can I help you?" asked the attractive and bubbly young lady.

"Yes, I'd like to see some recent newspapers. Can you direct me?"

"Yes, follow me," she said. "They are right over here. If you need any help, I will be happy to assist you."

"Okay," Noah said, "I should be fine."

The most recent papers were hung on rods, making them easy to access. Several older gentlemen sat around at different tables and in overstuffed chairs, reading, just like you might expect to see them in their homes. It was a comfortable and relaxed setting. He needed that after a five-hour drive. Sorting through the papers, he quickly found Monday's. His eyes lit up, thinking it would surely have something of interest. He took it to his chair and read the headline.

"Local Man Killed in Robbery Attempt"

He could not read fast enough to satisfy his curiosity; he had to slow down and concentrate. The paper soon made it clear that Bon had no wife or living children. He and his wife had divorced, and their only son did not return from the war. The paper even gave the man's address. Noah could not wait to see where the home was and if there was any activity there, so he put the newspaper back and moved quickly toward the door and back to his black Ford Focus.

Following the sometimes-windy road up Tiner's Hill, he found himself directly in front of the smallish, one-story, clapboard home in need of a lot of attention. The white paint was peeling. Weeds had taken over what once was landscaping. It looked empty, so Noah pulled into the grassy, gravel driveway and stopped. Sitting there, he pondered if it would be possible to get in. He speculated about what might be lying around and what that might tell him.

He waited a few minutes, and no other vehicles came by. Noah had never broken the law before, but this felt different. He needed to make sure there was nothing that would incriminate Little Joe. It looked so easy.

In the back of the house, he found another entrance. He considered trying to open it, but, more immediately, he felt the need to relieve himself of his morning coffee. Stepping closer to the back wall, he unzipped his pants and began urinating. He thought about his aim. At one time, there was landscaping here and a man who lived inside. Now, having seen that same man die, he found himself watering the man's overgrown weeds. If only that man had stayed home and cared for his property, everything would have been different.

After answering nature's call, Noah tried the door. It was locked. On the right side of the small porch was a flowerpot. He reached down and lifted it up, exposing a hidden key he half expected to be there. The key slid into the tarnished brass lock easily, and he turned it. Slowly, he pushed the creaking door open. A rush of nerves grabbed him, and his hands trembled. He knew he should turn and run, but he couldn't resist going farther until, finally, he was more inside than out. Looking around, he saw crooked pictures of family on the walls and the older-style table and chairs in the kitchen. He walked across the worn carpet on the living room floor; it was the life Bon had failed to live. The allure of gold caused him to forget the things most important in life. He once had everything a man could need, but greed left him restless and unsatisfied. Noah thought about how much happier he would have been if he had just taken care of the life he had. And, he might still be alive.

Noah searched for a box or bin that might hold pictures and mementos. From room to room, he walked, looking for anything that would give others a clue as to what the man was up to. He searched the cramped bedroom closet and peered under the unmade twin-size bed. Then he spotted another door. It was another closet. High on a shelf sat a metal box, roughly the size of two shoeboxes. Noah stretched as far as he could to reach it and bring it down. He had not seen anything else, so instead of lingering, he took the box with him out the back door. Now feeling his nerves again, he shook while he locked the door behind him. He carefully placed the key back where he found it. He hurried to his car. He had no sooner reached to open his door when he heard another car coming. He quickly shoved the box inside, on the seat, and stood erect, as though he was just looking the place over. As the car came closer, he turned to see who it was. Rounding the bend was a black and white patrol car with the words "Johnson City Police" written across the side.

Noah reached into his car and covered the box with the Johnson City Tribune paper he had bought in the hotel lobby. He remained by the car as the patrol vehicle pulled into the driveway beside his black Ford Focus.

"What are you doing here?" asked the officer.

"I'm just looking the place over, officer."

"Do you know the owner?"

"No, sir, I don't. But I read he died in the paper. Thought I'd check to see if the place was worth buying." Noah said.

Just then, a call came over the police radio monitor. They were needed to investigate an accident in town.

"I want you to get off this property and stay off until you see a for-sale sign in the yard. Do you understand?" said the officer.

"Yes, sir, officer," replied Noah. "I'm leaving now!"

Noah pulled away, grateful for the call that ended the officer's questioning. He decided he did not want to be linked with the dead man's home. He wanted to go back to his room and go through the box, but he felt he should quickly travel the fifty-nine miles to the border and be out of Tennessee. Having left his bag at the hotel, he had no choice. He carefully drove the speed limit, not wanting another run-in with the law. Cautiously, he made his way to the hotel. Noah wondered, *Did they take down his license number? Would there be police at the hotel when he got there?* His nerves were getting the best of him, but he had no choice; he could not leave his bag. Seeing no police cars at the hotel, he quickly gathered his things and headed to the front desk.

"Leaving early, sir?" said the clerk.

"Yes, change of plans."

"I'm sorry you have to leave. Was everything okay?"

"Everything was fine. I just had a change of plans."

"Everything's squared away. Y'all come back and see us soon."

"I don't think so," Noah said and left as quickly as possible.

Noah drove to the border like a model citizen, careful and alert. He didn't want to see any more police. Maybe he could make it home without needing another stop. But if he had to stop, it would be in the next state. Tennessee had seen the last of him–or so he hoped.

Chapter 10

The Tin Box of a Tattered Life

As Noah drove toward the Tennessee border, he kept a closer eye on the rearview mirror than the road ahead. When he finally passed the 'Welcome to North Carolina' sign, the muscles in his back began to relax. It was four-thirty in the afternoon, and he hadn't eaten in hours. Tired and hungry, he scanned the roadside for a restaurant.

He began thinking of Little Joe. Could his memory loss include forgetting where he hid the gold? The thought struck him like a lightning bolt. He'd never considered that possibility until now. What if Little Joe didn't even remember the gold existed? Worse, what if he remembered it but had no idea where he'd hidden it? Noah could only hope that Little Joe's mind would recall everything except Bon's invasion of his home. Questions churned in his mind. How much more tangled could this web become? A familiar adage surfaced: "Oh, what a tangled web we weave, when first we practice to deceive."

A road sign read, "Gas, Three Miles Ahead." Another advertised a Wendy's. He was glad, at last, to have a chance to eat.

After refueling, Noah drove across the street to Wendy's. Parking the car, he went inside to order. The smell of coffee alone began to soothe his frayed nerves. Seated with his meal, he pulled out his iPhone to check for messages. Three texts from Aileen popped up:

"Where are you?

I tried to call you.

Why don't you answer?"

Noah realized he'd silenced his phone earlier at the library. Feeling a pang of guilt, he checked his voicemail and saw a message from Aileen. Instead of listening to it, he decided to call her back immediately.

"Hello," said Aileen.

"Hi, how is everyone doing?"

"Everything is fine. How are you? What's going on?"

"Oh, I'll tell you all about it when I get back."

"Where are you, in a hotel?" she said.

"No, I left Johnson City. I'm on my way back–somewhere in South Carolina right now. I may get a room for the night, and might not. Might just come home. Where are you?"

"Mom and I are in our hotel room. She is just leaving to go back to the hospital with Dad."

"I forgot that I turned my phone off at the library, so I didn't get your messages until now. If everything is all right, I'll call you again after I finish eating."

"Okay, I'll be here," she said.

A full belly solved one of his problems. Now, he had to decide whether to drive home or get a room for the night. He had nearly 265 miles to go—about a four-and-a-half-hour drive. But he had been going since seven a.m. and was tired. He probably wouldn't get there until nine or ten o'clock.

He finally decided to drive another hour or so, then find a hotel and rest. That way, he'd only have a three-hour drive in the morning and could get home early. Grabbing a coffee to go, he slid back into his black Ford Focus and merged onto the highway, heading south.

As he drove, Noah's mind replayed the day's events. He thought about the legal ramifications if he were found out. His career would be over. He would never again be trusted if something like this made the papers. He had risked so much and was lucky he wasn't caught. Calmer now, he admitted a hard truth: he wasn't cut out to be a criminal. He increasingly realized how right Little Joe had been—the gold, for all its beauty and mysterious allure, was also a terrible burden.

The sky shifted from bright blue to a foreboding gray, and soon, rain began to fall. At first, the droplets fell slowly, but they quickly turned into large, heavy splashes that smacked against his windshield. Moments later, the storm intensified, pelting the car with billions of relentless raindrops. The heavy downpour blurred the road ahead. He spotted a motel sign at the next exit and took it as a good reason to stop for the night.

In his motel room, Noah watched out the window at the growing storm. He was glad he was able to get off the road when he did. It wasn't a nice motel, but it was comfortable–smaller than the one he'd stayed in that morning.

After a hot shower, he called Aileen to check in.

"I'll spend the night here and leave early in the morning," he said.

"How is your room?" she asked.

"It's so small I could use the bathroom and answer the front door at the same time."

"Oh, wow! I wouldn't try stretching yourself that far." She laughed.

"Did you learn much in Johnson City?"

"Well, yes. He wasn't married and didn't have any children. I know that much. I found his home, and it was pretty run-down. I doubt he had many friends, given the way he lived. I'll tell you all about it when I get home. How are your mom and dad doing?"

"They're doing great! Dad is getting stronger every day. Mom is much more relaxed now than she was."

"That's good to hear. Is your dad remembering anything?"

"No, not much change there."

"Well, okay. I'm going to sign off. I need some coffee– or maybe a beer if I can find one. I want to relax and get some sleep."

"Okay, let me know when you get back on the road tomorrow," Aileen said.

"Will do. Goodnight, hon, love you."

"Love you too, goodbye!"

Noah ended the call and plugged his phone into a charger. Looking out the window again, he noticed lights across the street. Squinting through the rain, he realized it might be a convenience store. A twenty-four-ounce beer sounded better than coffee. He held a plastic garbage bag over his head and ran to the car. He was right- just across the street, there was a gas station with a small convenience store.

"Do you have any beer?" Noah asked the small, friendly lady behind the counter.

"Sure do," she replied in a typical South Carolina twang, her smile warm and calming. "Right back there," she said, pointing toward the rear of the store.

As Noah followed her gesture, he found himself oddly comforted by her accent. It reminded him that life was beginning to feel normal again, and normal was exactly what he craved.

"I'll take this," he said, grabbing a twenty-four-ounce Bud Light from the cooler."

"Will that be all?"

"No, give me one of those Powerball tickets too," he said on impulse.

Leaving the store, Noah wondered why he'd bought a ticket that required luck–especially when his father-in-law had a fortune in hidden gold. Despite all his study of the human mind, there were still times he didn't understand his own.

The rain had let up some, though he still needed the wipers on low as he drove back to the motel. He pulled up to his room, shoved the gearshift into park, and reached for the paper bag holding his beer. As his gaze shifted, his eyes landed on the Johnson City Press lying on the passenger seat–suddenly, he remembered the box he'd taken from Bon's residence. It had completely slipped his mind until now. Grabbing the box along with his beer, Noah stepped out into the drizzle. Near the office, a group of boys stood huddled in the rain, talking animatedly. He wondered why anyone would be standing in the rain but didn't linger. Once inside the room, safe and dry, Noah set the box on the bed and opened the beer. The tab cracked with a satisfying hiss, and he took a long, deep swig. It tasted like more. He knew calmness lay at the bottom of the can, and for now, that was enough.

Slipping off his 'Counselor's Do it on a Couch' T-shirt, Noah couldn't stop staring at the box. He wondered how he could have forgotten it and pondered what it might contain. Would it answer all of his questions? Would it finally put all of his fears to rest? He contemplated the possibilities. Taking another gulp of beer, he felt the coolness of it in his throat. His mind raced as he took the box in his hands, gently, like it held some mystical power. He carried it to a small desk in the corner, set it gently under the dim lamp, and pulled up the creaky chair. The hinges squeaked as he lifted the lid–a sound straight out of a bad thriller movie. The smell of mildew wafted up, unpleasant and sharp. On top lay an old newspaper clipping, yellowed and brittle. The headline read, "Pinkerton Man Found Murdered." It was a write-up about a murder that took place long ago. It looked like a library film reel copy. A stack of letters, bound with a brittle gum band, sat in one corner of the box. He picked them up and set them aside for later. Beneath the letters were envelopes containing black-and-white photographs, their edges curling with age. A deed to a house, stamped "PAID IN FULL," rested underneath the photos, along with a deck of playing cards featuring scenes from Las Vegas on their backs. Another newspaper clipping stuck out from the pile, this one headlined: "Couple Recite Nuptials in Moonlight Marriage."

Noah went through the contents quickly, hoping anything of importance would jump out at him, but nothing did. He took another drink from his twenty-four-ounce Bud Light, then another. He thought, *this beer might be the best part of my night.* He considered dumping the contents onto the bed for a better look but didn't want the smell getting into the covers. He looked in the closet and found a plastic laundry bag. He would place each item in the bag after examining it to keep things organized.

Among the papers, a folded parcel map caught his eye. It appeared to be from the Johnson City tax office, showing homes on Tiner's Hill and listing their owners. Noah squinted at the names, but the beer and the long day dulled his focus.

As he drained the last of his twenty-four-ounce Bud Light, a wave of calm finally settled over him. The tension that had clung to him all day faded into a pleasant haze. His eyelids grew heavy, and his motivation to continue sifted away. He found the calmness he had wished for all day. He lay across the bed and embraced the inevitable dream world. Whatever truths the box held would have to wait. For now, he let the promise of dreams and the temporary escape of rest take him. Morning would bring new light and, hopefully, new clarity.

***

Noah rose with the sun Tuesday morning. He stretched briefly and made his way to the bathroom. The beer from the night before had done its job–he felt rested and refreshed, his body lighter than it had been in days. After brushing his teeth and washing his face, he wondered if the store across the street was open. They would have coffee. Back in the main room, he once again gazed at the tin box of mementos. Seeing it reminded him why he was there. There was still a job to be done. He could do it now or later. Noah decided to get coffee before making up his mind. Coffee and a donut would clear his head, he thought.

Outside, the rain had stopped, and the sun was rising prominently in the clear blue sky. It wasn't the view from Little Joe's, but it was still a lovely morning. The air smelled clean, the world washed fresh by the storm.

Entering the store, he saw a new face on the register. She was much younger, of average height, her blond hair neatly pulled back, her warm smile radiating friendliness.

"Good morning!" she said with a cheerful Southern drawl. "How y'all doin'?"

"I'm fine, thank you," Noah replied. "Just need some coffee."

"Is that all you need?" she said, her smile widening slightly.

"Maybe one of these donuts," he added, picking out his favorite blueberry-flavored donut, with no icing, from the clear plastic display case near the counter.

After paying the attendant, he returned to his little room. He found himself smiling and anticipating his hot coffee and donut. Then he remembered the tin box. He wanted to get home early, but now was the perfect time to go through it in private.

Back in his room, he sat down at the desk with his coffee and thought about that tin and all he had been through. He had a feeling something inside was waiting to be discovered. After eating his donut, he began going through the box. On the bottom, he found an old, stained Tiparillo cigar box. Inside were more pictures. The photos were of men and women; their faces faded with time—probably relatives. Beneath the photos was an open envelope addressed to Michael Bon; the return address read Lydia Bon. Lydia Bon, he remembered, was Bon's estranged wife. The postmark was fairly recent. He gently removed the letter from the plain envelope and began to read.

Dear Michael,

I pray this letter finds you well. I know you're angry with me, but I hope you can understand why I left.

You became completely absorbed in the past and refused to live in the present. You had too great an obsession with treasure and no concern for making a home for us. It finally made living with you impossible.

I know you meant well. I heard the stories so many times I could scream. I know them all by heart. But did you ever hear one word of my concerns? No, you never heard me. I tried to make a home for us, but you didn't seem to care. Always dreaming of fictional treasure—and never the little band of gold you promised me. The one I never got.

You never had time. You didn't have time for your responsibilities. Never time to make needed repairs on the house. No time for me.

I loved you, Michael. I would have done anything for you. I did so want to be the gold in your life, but I clearly did not shine enough for you.

I'm not writing to condemn you. I know you meant well, and I don't have hard feelings. I'm writing because I need to tell you something. Something I can't keep to myself any longer.

I am dying, Michael.

The doctor says it is kidney disease. I need a transplant, but my insurance will not cover it. Since I don't have the money, I'm sunk. The doctor told me I should put my affairs in order. Since you are my only affair, I thought you should know. He didn't know when exactly, but not long, I'm told.

I want you to know I understand. I forgive you, and I hope you'll forgive me. I promise to only remember the good times from now on. But please, don't waste your life. Live it! Real gold can be found in the moments of each and every day.

My fondest farewell,

Lydia

Now, Noah understood why Michael had done what he did. He needed money, and he was out of time. It was a last-ditch effort. He wanted the money for his ex-wife's surgery and was so desperate that he would kill for it.

Noah sat looking at the letter and thinking she probably didn't even know that he was dead. Bon no longer seemed like a crazed gunman to Noah, but a sad, desperate, and broken man. He had as good a reason as anyone could have for doing what he did. Noah thought about having tackled him in Little Joe's office and the pounding he had wanted to give him. Now, he felt different. Now, he actually felt sorry for Bon. For the first time, he understood the weight of the secret he shared with Little Joe. How could anything be worth more than the two lives already lost?

Satisfied, he knew all he needed to know. Noah loaded the tin box with all its contents into the trunk of the car, grabbed his clothes, and put them in the back seat. He looked at the store across the street and then the little motel. So, this is what it feels like to be helpless. I will never forget this day or this place, as long as I live.

He had done his detective work and found everything he was looking for. There was no further danger to his family. But now, his life had touched another's, and it was complicated.

That morning, the road was nearly empty. Noah set his cruise control to sixty-five miles per hour. The sound of the tires rolling over the pavement seemed louder than usual. But he was comfortable and relaxed. His mind was heading in a different direction than usual. His thoughts felt clearer than they had in days, and for once, he felt in control. There was clarity to his thinking that made him feel more in charge than usual. He, like Little Joe, embraced the mind's abilities. They knew to give it free rein, to be creative, and to trust the results. Noah thought about Lydia and the money she needed. Though they didn't know one another, he felt sorry for her.

He thought about the gold and how it could cause so much suffering. Gold is just currency, he thought. Money is a tool to be used. Leaving it hidden is a waste. But converting it to cash, though desirable, would not be easy.

The money–and the problem–belonged to them both. The Napoleon Hill equation kept rolling through his head, 'transmute the intangible thought process of desire into its tangible monetary equivalent.' Allow your brain to vibrate on a higher frequency, and the answer will come.

He mentally listed the problems. They had the gold, but it could not be converted to cash. It had a larger numismatic value than bar gold. Its age and place of origin might be recognized by an expert dealer. Perhaps one could go through a collector rather than a dealer. Either way, it would raise questions.

Noah remembered reading that the first step to achieving any sound goal is to state your purpose clearly and decisively. It is very important to write down and be specific. You must repeat your stated intent over and over until your subconscious mind adopts it as its own. Then allow your subconscious time to cultivate the idea and find the solution.

He thought the surgery might cost around sixty to seventy thousand dollars. Even if he had the money, he couldn't just hand it to a stranger without raising suspicion. This part would no doubt take some thought.

He spotted a blue rest area sign and pulled over to write down his stated intent.

He wrote:

I will seek Little Joe's approval and learn where the gold is hidden. I will find a way to convert it to cash. I will find a way to help Lydia pay for her surgery. Once these are done, I will donate a large sum to the Shriners Children's Hospital and invest in home security for our families.

Noah hoped this would be enough to put his subconscious mind to work. Now he needed only to repeat the command, finish his drive, and wait for the answers. That's how it worked for Little Joe. Maybe it would work for him.

The miles flew past, but his thoughts moved even faster. He remembered a friend who had a gold and silver shop in Pennsylvania. Ted had been in the business of buying and selling gold collectibles for fifty years. Noah could ask Ted the questions without having any gold to show him. The answers he received would help him understand the situation better and probably give him other ideas. The principles were working; the answers would come.

Chapter 11

The Subconscious Mind

As he drove, Noah reflected on the principles outlined in Think and Grow Rich by Napoleon Hill. These were the principles Little Joe lived by. Those, and the Bible. They had worked for him. He became very successful over the years, without needing a winning lottery ticket or buried treasure. He lived his life by the numbers, and he had faith.

The book emphasized faith, saying, "faith is the lead chemist of the mind. When faith is mixed with the vibration of desire, the subconscious mind instantly picks up that vibration. It is then sent to Infinite Intelligence and translated into a spiritual equivalent."

He considered how the subconscious mind stores both negative and positive thoughts. That you may voluntarily plant any plan or desire in your mind, and it can be translated into its material or monetary equivalent. The book claimed there was ample evidence supporting the belief that the subconscious mind serves as a link between man's finite mind and Infinite Intelligence. It functioned like an intermediary, through which one could draw upon the forces of boundless intellect. It described a secret process by which mental impulses are transformed into their spiritual equivalent. It stated that the only way to convert prayer into reality was to transmit it to a source capable of answering it.

He wondered if this is how some people strayed down the wrong path–entertaining base desires instead of those that led to success. He had read that while you can't fully control the subconscious mind, you can submit any proposal you wish to transform into reality. It acts on dominant desires–those mixed with emotion and faith.

The book repeated that ample evidence supports the belief that the subconscious mind connects man's finite mind with Infinite Intelligence. It is like an intermediary through which one can draw upon the forces of boundless intellect. The secret process where mental impulses are transformed into their spiritual equivalent.

He marveled at the creative potential of the subconscious mind, so vast and mysterious it inspired awe.

Little Joe had told him that reading the book once was not enough. "You only retain ten percent of what you read." He had said. To absorb its contents, you might need to read it ten times. And of course, apply the principles it teaches.

The more he thought about it, the less important the physical gold seemed. Tapping into the mind's treasure seemed far more exciting.

After his talk with Little Joe, Noah read a few articles about the lost Confederate Gold. It was fascinating–many believed gold was still out there, scattered between Georgia and Washington, D.C. The Confederacy had sold cotton to Mexico, acquiring thirty-nine kegs of Mexican silver dollars. These, too, were transported to Danville, Virginia, and never seen again.

He read accounts suggesting that others had taken portions of the treasure. President Jefferson Davis transferred eighty-six thousand dollars in gold to bonded Confederate officials James A. Semple and his assistant, Edward Tidball. They were tasked with delivering it to the Confederate government's financial agent in Liverpool, the commercial house of Fraser, Trenholm & Company.

Postmaster General John Reagan, who had accompanied Davis in Danville, claimed the gold was hidden in the false bottomed carriage.

Semple and Tidball disappeared for a time. Soon after, Tidball resurfaced up in Winchester, Virginia, where he built an elaborate house, which he called *Linden Farm*. He became a prominent citizen and was later elected to the Virginia House of Delegates. Tidball's elaborate home and growing properties made it likely he had profited from the disbursement of the Confederate treasury.

Noah also read that during a renovation of the *Linden Farm*, a hidden document was discovered in a wall, confirming Tidball's possession of part of the gold

Even the infamous Jesse James, who in his earlier years fought for the Confederacy, was suspected of hiding Confederate gold. He was rumored to be a member of a secretive Confederate group: the Knights of the Golden Circle. Clearly, Little Joe was not alone.

Noah's subconscious continued feeding him the knowledge he sought. He contemplated what would happen if he told his secret. Surely, the United States Government would swoop in and take it all, just like they had in 1865. Maybe he could give them a little but keep most of it. "Show just enough to the world to get paid for the movie rights," he thought." "Yeah, hell yeah, there would be a book and a movie and the 'Late Night Show' and tons of press, then find a private collector to buy the rest. Profits from the book and movie could offset the loss from selling the rest under the table. In the end, the gold would be gone, and there would be no more Michael Bons to worry about. Everything would be out in the open.

Better yet, unload most of it before the newspapers broke the story. After they do, you won't have to do anything. Once the whole world is watching, all you'll have to do is smile.

The ideas were coming fast, and Noah was impressed. The mind was truly a wonderful place to live. Still, one question loomed large: Who would buy the gold?

He pulled his car off the highway, grabbed his phone and called the only person he could think of who might help. Ted Young owned *'Youngs Gold & Silver'* in Rochester, Pennsylvania. He bought and sold precious metals.

"Hello, Ted,"

"Hello," came the voice at the other end. "What can I do for you?"

"Ted, it's me, Noah. I have a question."

"Oh. Hi, Noah. What do you need?"

"I might know a guy who has some very old gold coins to sell. He is looking for a collector or private buyer for a large sum."

"How large?"

"Strictly between us–a very large amount. He wants to keep it discreet."

"I may know a couple of people. I'll talk to them and see how interested they are. What dates are they?"

"Somewhere between 1861 to 1865, as best I know. Confederate."

"Wow, I would really like to see one of those. I'll get back to you."

As he pulled back onto the road, Noah felt a surge of relief–things were finally coming together. But he had not spoken to Little Joe about his plan, and Little Joe might be against it. At least he was working on a firm plan, and he would have to appreciate that much. Then again, Noah had no idea what Little Joe knew or didn't know at that point. It was time to call Aileen again.

"Hello, where are you at, Noah?" Aileen answered.

"I'm on my way. Another two hours or so, and I'll be there. How are your mom and dad doing?"

"They're fine."

"Is your dad talking much?"

"Yes, he seems fine. His memory is still spotty."

"That's what I was wondering. I hope he will get well soon."

"We all do," Aileen said.

"Do me a favor, will you? Tell your dad that I said, 'If I were a dog, I'd be a golden retriever, weary of sitting on the porch.' It's an inside joke kind of thing. Let me know what he says."

"Well, that doesn't make any sense, but I wrote it down, and I will tell him. I'll see him in just a few minutes."

"Also, tell him I'm taking care of things, and I won't let him down."

"Okay, I'll tell him."

"Okay, hon. I'll get off here because I'm driving; talk to you later."

"Okay, bye."

Noah thought about what he had said and hoped Little Joe would understand. It wasn't long before Aileen was calling back.

Dad said to tell you, "If you can't run with the big dogs, stay on the porch." He said when he gets out of there, you guys can run together.

Noah laughed aloud. "He knows exactly what I mean. That's great! Thanks, honey."

"Alright, you guys keep your secrets. I'm not 'too' curious."

"Won't be long–you'll understand."

"Okay, Big Dog, you drive safe and get home soon."

"I will see you soon. Goodbye," Noah said.

"Bye," Aileen replied.

Noah felt much better. Little Joe's answer told him he remembered the gold and understood what he meant. He would be able to talk to him soon about his plan. It seemed like a load had been lifted from him. So much had changed since Monday morning.

So many things had happened, so much to remember, so important to think clearly and succinctly. The solution to all their problems could be answered with a single phone call from Ted.

Noah repeated his mental affirmations, clinging to the faith that his prayers would be answered. In his mind, he pictured everything working out exactly as he planned. He would find a buyer for the gold, and Little Joe would write the story. He would sell the movie rights. He could already feel the nerves of walking onto the *'Tonight Show'* stage. He could see them helping Lydia get her life-changing surgery. It was as though it had already happened. The commands were in place. The visualization was working. He had faith that everything would happen soon.

The traffic became hectic when nearing high-population areas. Noah took note of it and wondered who had been driving. He could not recall anything for the past fifty miles. His mind was elsewhere. Yet he drove without error. Clearly, his subconscious had taken the wheel during his mental absence. As he thought about this curious ability, the phone rang.

"Hello!"

"Noah, it's Ted."

"Hey, Ted. What did you find out?"

"I have a contact who'll do fifty cents on the dollar. I'll take ten percent."

"I'll pass it along, but don't sit on your hands—this is a once-in-a-lifetime chance."

"It's not that bad, Noah. There are problems with buying things like this."

"Well, let me know what your man says."

Noah said, "I will." And hung up.

He wasn't thrilled with the offer—but maybe it wasn't as bad as it first sounded. Fifty percent of something is better than one hundred percent of nothing. He wondered, for the first time, how much it was. That would make a huge difference. He had been thinking it was a lot, but what is a lot? He also considered the dilemma of hidden money–money you can't spend without raising suspicion. Hidden money can't be spent. At least they had an offer. That was big. He had come a long way since that morning. Little Joe was getting better, and the solution was coming.

A sign read, 'Charleston – 50 Miles.' Noah was happy to see that sign. Fifty miles was nothing. He would be home in an hour. What a day!

Homeward Bound

Diane and Aileen sat at Little Joe's bedside as his personal physician examined him. Dr. Guffey had a youthful appearance with thick black hair slightly graying.

"Mr. McCurdy," he said with a boyish grin, "You've been with us for five days and have shown remarkable improvement. I don't see any reason why you cannot go home. Do you have any stairs at home that would make it difficult for you to get around?"

"No, sir. My home is all on one floor."

"You will have to take it easy until I see you again. No lifting, nothing strenuous, and get plenty of rest. I will have to see you again in a few days for a follow-up. I believe you might recover even more quickly at home. Now, your memory is still a little sketchy, but we think it will gradually return." He adjusted his glasses and made notes on his iPad. "Do you have any questions?"

"No, doctor. I feel fine. I'm a little sore, but I think I can get around okay."

"Excellent. I'll fill out the paperwork for your release. You can get dressed; the hospital will send a wheelchair for you. Call my receptionist tomorrow and make an appointment to come in for a checkup next week."

"Okay, Doc. Will do!"

Aileen left the room so that Little Joe could get dressed. Diane stayed to help him pack his things.

"Bet you're glad to be going home," she said.

"I can't wait to get home. Can't wait to relax by the pool. That reminds me–I forgot to ask the doctor about swimming. I suppose I can wade into the water if I don't try to swim, huh? That shouldn't hurt anything."

"You don't want to get your bandages wet, Diane cautioned. "If you have any open wounds, they could become infected."

"No, I think I'm all patched up. Still, we'll double-check before we leave. Where did Aileen go?"

"She took some things to the car. She'll be back," Diane said.

"Good. I want to stop on the way and pick up some pizza. I have been dying for some of Al's Pizza."

"We can do that. I'll call ahead and have them make one up for you," Diane said.

He had endured confinement because he had no choice—but now, knowing he was free to leave, anticipation bubbled inside him. Time moved slowly; he looked again to see if the minute hand was moving.

Dressed and ready to go, he sat on the side of his bed, wondering when his ride would get there. He stared out the window at the blue skies and sunshiny afternoon awaiting him. He would be free soon. Free to do as he pleased, within limits. Excitement grew in him as he waited.

A short, middle-aged woman entered his room with a wheelchair.

"Are you leaving us, Mr. McCurdy?"

"I sure am! Just as fast as I can. Are you my ride?"

"Yes, I am. Do you need any help getting into the chair?"

"Nope. I'm good."

"Well then, hop in, and I'll take you to the entrance. Your daughter is bringing your car around. She'll meet us there."

With all his belongings loaded onto his chair with him, they moved way too slowly for his liking. At the front doors, they saw Aileen pulling up.

"That's good, thank you," he said, lifting himself out of the wheelchair. I can handle it from here,"

Diane opened the front door for him.

"You can ride shotgun, Joe. I'll jump into the back," she said.

"Stop on the way at Al's Pizza, Aileen. Your father is craving it, and when he wants pizza, only Al's will do. I ordered a large for us to pick up."

"Oh, okay. That sounds good."

"I'm not in any hurry now, ladies." Little Joe said, relaxing in his seat. I'm just glad to get out of that place. It is so nice to see something other than those four walls. Take your time, hon–I'm just enjoying the ride."

Pulling into his driveway reminded Little Joe of what put him in the hospital; he felt a pang of regret and sorrow. He wondered if the stigma of that night would ever go away. The ghastly images would surely test the mind's power to suppress and reshape the darkness. Then again, maybe a guy shouldn't forget something so powerful, even if it is ugly. Like the way he used his memory of having lung cancer to drive him to work harder, knowing his life was a gift or miracle that should be earned. He needed to be productive to feel he deserved his reprieve. Only time would tell.

"Where is Noah?" he asked. "Has anyone heard from him today?"

"Yes, he should be getting here pretty soon," Aileen reassured him.

"Good. I'll be glad to see him. We need this family together."

"He'll be here," Aileen said. "Mind if I drive across the lawn and drop you off by the pool, Dad?"

"Yeah, that's okay."

"Then I'll get you some iced tea to go with your pizza."

"Good idea. Your mom can help me to my chair and take my things in through that door."

Being home again was like a tonic. He loved this home, the view of the ocean, the soothing sound of the waves rolling ashore. It was why he'd chosen to live here. Now, surrounded by the people he loved most, it felt like the best medicine in the world.

Soon, Little Joe was joined poolside by Diane and Aileen. Curious about its condition, Little Joe asked about his office.

Diane said. "The police did not tell me until yesterday that we were allowed back in. I hired a cleaning service- they should be here in the morning. Until then, I think it's best you stay out of there."

His memory of that evening was spotty; a lot of negative thoughts blipped through his mind. He understood from speaking to the police and Diane that it was a mess in there. He was anxious to be able to use it again but apprehensive at the same time. He had been told what happened. Now, when he thought of his room, it was like he had been violated. Little Joe's sanctum sanctorum had been defiled. Even his most optimistic place now carried a shadow. He didn't like the feeling. Soon, he would go back and face its mystery head-on.

It was not long before they heard Noah pull in. Aileen ran to greet him. Little Joe and Diane were glad to have him back as well.

"I gave Addie two days off because we weren't going to be here," Diane said. "I'd better go in and see what I can find to go with that pizza, maybe a salad. Will you give me a hand, Aileen? Anything special you want?" she asked Little Joe.

"No, whatever you come up with is fine. I'm not really hungry, but Noah will be."

Noah sat across from Little Joe, pouring himself a frosted glass of Diane's iced tea. The ocean view, the smell of chlorine from the pool, and the sweet lemony taste of Diane's iced tea told him he was home again.

"Tell me about your trip, Noah. What have you been up to?"

"I was worried, sir, worried there may be others who know our secret and may come to pay us a visit. I didn't want any more surprises. I left for Johnson City Monday morning and did some checking around."

"What did you learn?"

"I think I know why that man did what he did. And I'm pretty sure nobody else was involved. He was a loner-lived alone, and didn't seem to have many friends. His wife had left him some time ago, and his son had died. He was just a sad, broken man who needed money."

"Why do you say he needed money?" Little Joe asked.

"Well," Noah began, "I found a letter from his ex-wife. She needs an expensive surgery and is not expected to live without it. He probably did it for her."

"That's heartbreaking. I wish I could talk to him now," Little Joe said.

"You tried to talk to him, sir, but he wasn't rational. There were very few choices."

"Do you think I did the right thing, Noah?"

"I thought so then, and still believe you had no choice. It was unfortunate he would not listen to reason. He brought it upon himself," Noah said.

"How did you gather all this information?"

"That's a story for another time, sir. I'm too tired to go into it now. But there is one other thing, I don't like keeping this secret from my wife. I don't feel good about it at all, sir."

"Noah, you're welcome to tell her, but not tonight. She'll have a million questions, and I'm too exhausted to handle them all. Let's wait until tomorrow. Just make sure she understands how important secrecy is. Total discretion—no exceptions!"

"I understand, sir."

Noah was glad to be back, and doubly so, now that Little Joe was home again and doing well. He was not alone with his secret anymore. Little Joe was back in charge of it. Though little had changed, a load had been lifted from him. He felt relaxed and thought the most important thing to do next was to hug his wife again, the kind of hug that tells her she's the only thing that matters.

"One thing, Noah," Little Joe said with a grin on his face.

"What's that, sir?" Noah responded, more curious about the grin than the answer.

"You did a great job while I was out of sorts. I'm grateful to you and, well, I could not be prouder."

"Thank you, sir. I was proud to be of service, and I'm sure glad you're back!"

Diane grilled two hamburgers, topping them with fresh tomatoes, onions, and lettuce for Noah. The early evening sun was setting behind the house, creating even more shade on their table. With kind, sweet words, the smell of great food, and smiles all around, they bent their elbows and filled their bellies.

Life seemed normal again, at least for a little while.

Chapter 12

Questions & Answers

Little Joe was right. When Noah told Aileen about the gold, she called him a liar.

"That is the craziest story I've ever heard. My dad did not tell you that!"

"Yes, he did!" "Noah shot back. "That's what all this has been about. That man came here to rob your dad because he knew about it. That's what he wanted."

"How could he have known about it when I didn't?"

"That's another long story. Your dad was right."

"What do you mean?"

"He said you would have a million questions. He said he was too weak to answer them all. It's quite an amazing story, and it is hard to believe. But it's true. I haven't seen it, and I don't know where it's hidden, but he told me about it before that Bon guy showed up. When I went to Bon's house, I found proof."

"I don't even know how to process this, Noah. It's all just too much all at once."

"I understand. I was shocked too–but everything will be okay. We will talk it over tomorrow, and once everything is out in the open, we can decide what we want to do about it."

"If Dad wasn't hurting, I would go right over there and wake him up!"

"Better sleep on it, hon. He'll be more up for questions tomorrow."

Aileen tossed and turned for an hour before asking, "Noah, are you asleep? I wonder if Mom knows?"

"I honestly don't know," he replied drowsily.

"Can't wait until tomorrow. Goodnight, hon," she whispered.

"Goodnight," Noah replied.

Noah's trip must have worn him out—it wasn't like him to sleep in. When he awoke, it was to the smell of coffee that Aileen had brought him.

"Oh, that smells wonderful," Noah said. "What time is it?" He grabbed his old watch from the nightstand and held it up until his eyes adjusted.

"It's after seven, dear. You missed the sunrise."

"Still beautiful out there," he said, taking his coffee with him to the window. "Are your mom and dad up?"

"No, not yet. I brought you a blueberry scone to have with your coffee. I know you like them."

"Oh, thanks."

Time dragged as they waited for Little Joe and Diane to stir. When they were sure everyone was up, Noah and Aileen went to the kitchen to get more coffee. Through the window, they saw Little Joe and Diane having theirs on the patio by the pool. Little Joe remained in his pajamas, while Diane was already dressed. Both seemed to be deep in thought. Noah wondered why. Aileen stopped at the kitchen window and looked out at her father.

"I can't believe Dad kept this secret from us all this time."

"I don't think he wanted to keep it a secret. That's how he found out about it, too," Noah said.

"What do you mean?"

"Just that, he did not learn about it until his mother, your grandmother, died. She left him a letter telling him where it was. That's what he told me."

"You mean Grandma Nanny knew about it?"

"Yes, she brought it from Tennessee when she married your grandfather."

"Gee! This story just keeps getting better and better," mumbled Aileen.

"Why are you so upset? There are worse things to discover than learning you have family gold."

"Gosh, you're right. Think about what we could do with all that money. You said he never told you where it was, right?"

"Yeah, I don't know where it is."

"I want to know where it is, and I want to see that letter."

"Well, take it easy on your dad. He has more guts than anyone I have ever known. You should have seen him face down that guy, and it hasn't been easy for him to keep this secret. He's had a rough week."

"I know. I'll let him finish his coffee before I attack him!" Aileen laughed.

"You're the soul of discretion, you are!" Noah chuckled.

Joining Diane and Little Joe on the patio, Aileen decided to let her dad tell her in his own time.

After they said "good morning," Diane asked if everyone slept well. Aileen said, "Yeah." Little Joe sat stoically in his white wicker, cushioned armchair. He gazed east out onto the ocean.

"Look out over that ocean. See the sunlight dancing on the water? Isn't that the most beautiful thing you have ever seen? Looking out there, you can forget you have problems. It's mesmerizing. I could gaze at it all day."

Everyone nodded in agreement.

"You can get lost in a vision like that," he said.

Diane, sitting on his left, reached over and touched his arm. Pulling it toward her, she laid her head down on his arm and burst into tears.

"Now, now, what's all this about?" Little Joe asked gently.

"I'm sorry, I think I've held up pretty well through all of this. But, but, the thought of losing you... I could have lost you."

Little Joe patted her head with his right hand and tried to calm her. "You're not getting rid of me that easily," he joked. "We're going to have a lot of years together yet. Everything is okay now, darling."

Their attention was distracted by the sound of Addie's car puttering up the driveway.

"That thing sounds like a *Rolls Canardly*," he said.

"What's a Rolls Canardly?" Diane asked.

"It rolls down the hill, but can hardly make it up the next." Little Joe laughed. "I think Addie needs a new car. You know she came to visit me in the hospital? I told you she loved me."

"Did she really?" Diane asked. "That was sure nice of her. I wondered if she would even come back after what happened."

"Yeah, I meant to tell you about her coming, but I must have forgotten. She's part of the family. I'll have to find her a new car. My cousin Ronnie up in Greeneville, Tennessee, buys cars at an auction at a decent price. I'll ask him to find her one."

"Wonder what kind of car she would want?" Diane asked.

"Anything will be an improvement over what she's driving now." Little Joe laughed.

Next came the sound of a truck pulling into the driveway.

"Oh my, I nearly forgot. It's the cleaning people for your office. I'll go meet them and show them what needs to be done," Diane said. She stood quickly and disappeared into the house.

Little Joe sat thinking it should be him cleaning his room. But deep down inside, he knew it was better if someone else did the dirty work. His job was to write and be productive. Negative thoughts should be avoided–they creep in and take over. Once given space in the subconscious, they multiply and block positive progress. He wanted to think of it as a place of peace and creativity. He wasn't eager to remember the terrible things that had happened there. And he wasn't sure how it would affect his work when he finally went back in there.

"Good morning, everyone," Addie said as she toted out a coffee carafe on a tray with a nice array of bakery sweets.

"How are you feeling this morning, Mr. Joe?"

"I'm much better, Addie. Much better. Thank you for asking."

"Anyone up for some ham and eggs this morning?" she asked.

"I'm good," Little Joe said.

"I would love some of your ham and eggs this morning," Noah said

"Me too," Aileen agreed, as she poured herself more coffee.

"I'll whip it up right away and bring Miss Diane a plate, too."

It wasn't long before Diane returned and had breakfast with them. The workers could not be heard as they cleaned inside Little Joe's soundproof room. Little Joe thought that was a good thing, but he wondered how long they would take. He wasn't used to having people around–or having to think about them. He liked his solitude.

Aileen asked her dad, "Can we talk about some things later? After the workers leave?"

"Sure, I know you have a lot of questions. I'm sorry you had to learn about this the way you did. It's not what I wanted, hon, honestly. We'll talk about that later."

"Noah, will you tell us what you found out?"

"Yes, sir. I wanted to find out who Bon was and why he did what he did, so I went to Johnson City. I started at the library and looked through old newspaper articles. I learned he had been married and divorced. He had a son who passed away, and he lived alone. Bon's address was in the article, too, so I drove out to see where he lived. The house was run-down, needing paint and repairs. Found a key under a flower pot at the back door, so I went in."

"My gosh, Noah, you actually went in there? Why would you do that?" Aileen scolded.

"That's the only way I was going to learn anything. The house sat secluded on a lonely road. I didn't see anyone else around, and the key was there. I had to see if it worked. When it did, well, I was already in. I moved through the house quickly and looked where folks usually hide things. I found an old tin box full of mementos. I figured that would offer the best clues possible, so I took it and got the heck out. Good thing I did because the cops showed up just as I put that box in the car. Scared the heck out of me."

"Why were the police there?" Diane asked.

"Well, I guess they were doing the same thing I was. They were investigating him. They asked me what I was doing, and I made an excuse like I was interested in the property, but they pretty much ran me off. They told me to stay away from that place. Then they received another call on their radio and had to leave, so I did, too. I didn't stop until I hit the South Carolina line. I'm sure glad they answered that call when they did!"

"Noah, you could have gotten into real trouble, you know that?" Aileen chided.

"Yes, I do. It scared me plenty. All I can say is, the good Lord was with me."

"Oh man, Noah, that was a close one. I'm glad nothing worse happened," Little Joe said. "What did you learn from the box?"

"I was worn out from driving, so I rented a room in South Carolina. I went through the box there and found a letter from his ex-wife. It was not dated long ago, so I assume it was on his mind. She needs a life-or-death surgery, and her insurance will not cover it. I'm afraid she is going to die. He knew that, and I think he wanted money for her. It's very sad when you think about it. I wish he had told us that instead of waving that gun around. Now she has no one."

"That's terrible," Aileen said. "But why here and why us?"

Noah focused on Little Joe and said, "This guy had been tracking and following your every move, sir. He had records of births, deaths, and everything in between. He had clippings from newspapers. He even received newspapers from your hometown. He would have shown up sooner or later. Maybe he never had the nerve until his ex-wife needed him. Maybe that's what drove him to it."

"Sounds that way, Noah," Little Joe lamented. "Very sad and a hard business, to be sure. Do you know what kind of surgery she needs, or what it might cost?"

"About seventy thousand."

"Wow, that's a lot of money!" Little Joe responded.

"I've got an idea—let's talk more once I know the details."

"Great, Noah. I hope it's a good one."

Chapter 13

Of Kith and Kin

Noah had a general idea of how his plan might work, but nothing concrete. There was much to do before it could succeed. He had talked to Ted several times and received varied responses, none of which seemed good enough.

The idea of presenting his plan to Little Joe made him nervous. What if he hated the idea? What if Aileen or Diane hated the idea? At first, it all seemed simple, but now the task seemed daunting. Why did I open my big mouth? he wondered.

All things being equal, it was a good plan, but when you're planning the division of someone else's money, all things are not equal. He would have to come up with a great way to present it to Little Joe. If he liked it, Noah could tell the others. Little Joe would most likely appreciate the effort and not be hard on him. After all, something had to be done, and he had the feeling Little Joe would agree.

The thought of all that gold being lost forever if Little Joe died, or the worry that someone else might come looking for it, was not attractive. He would call Ted that afternoon and offer him a higher percentage to motivate him.

Noah thought about the family he was working so hard to please. They were close, but each had their own unique personality.

*****

Diane went over everything she wanted to be done in Little Joe's room. She kept a close watch on the workers, making sure it was cleaned thoroughly and nothing of importance was disturbed. She was meticulous and liked everything done just right. She was a sweet and gentle person, honest and kind to a fault. But when you say you're going to do something, you had better do it. She let them know what she expected and kept a close eye on them as they worked.

Little Joe met Diane one hot summer day when they were both sixteen. She was standing in his parents' yard, waiting for her sister, who was dropping off some things. He was working in his father's garage across the street when he spotted her. She wore a white blouse and tight-fitting blue-and-white-striped slacks. The white pin stripes curved ever so nicely over her shapely figure. After a brief look and a swirl of curiosity, he rushed out the door and crossed the street.

When their eyes met, he felt a connection immediately. He knew she was the girl for him.

As she told it, his shirtless, tanned, sweaty, muscular body glistened in the summer sun.

That's how they told the story many times. There was no doubt they were still very much in love, even after forty-seven years of marriage. He was the romantic, while Diane was usually more reserved. She rarely offered praise but would gently point out flaws, helping him improve. Seeing her break down earlier was rare. Though he knew she loved him, she was not showy and was not prone to public displays of affection. Diane was selfless, very giving, discreet, proper, and a private person, and she was happy with Little Joe.

Noah had a deep appreciation for Little Joe and always treated him with great respect. He had lost his own father a few years prior, and Little Joe helped fill that void in his heart. It took some time for them to become close because his father-in-law was a private person. He never interfered in his children's lives, but was always there when they needed him.

Noah saw how he bore painful personal losses and continued to be optimistic. He would just work harder to keep his mind busy. When the loss of family left him lonelier than he had ever been, instead of quitting, he reinvented himself. He just kept plowing forward. Work was his way of escaping the tragedies in his life, but he never blocked out his family or friends. He liked people and was well known. He enjoyed playing pool and loved to sing. Travel was a passion of his, but it was his Christian faith and love of his Country that seemed to keep him grounded. He would eagerly debate anyone, insisting the Founding Fathers were Christians who based our laws on Christian principles. He believed the Declaration of Independence, the Constitution, and Christianity were the very foundations of America, without any one of which this nation could not stand. He often reminded people that the phrase

"Separation of Church and State" appears in none of the founding documents.

He liked to tell people that Protestantism, Catholicism, and Judaism are religions, but Christianity is a philosophy, and there is no separation of philosophy and state either.

Noah looked up to him and did not want to let him down.

In his wife, Aileen, Noah saw attributes of both her father and mother. Aileen had a somewhat upright bearing like her father. She tried hard to always do right and was a perfectionist when it came to her work. Reserved and somewhat shy yet very creative, she had a great love of reading and writing. Like her dad, she was an idealist. She was highly intelligent, witty, and compassionate toward others. Little Joe told everyone that she got her mother's good looks because he kept his. Then, he would laugh out loud.

Amber, her sister, was bold and determined, much like her grandmother, Macel. She did well in crowds, had the gift of gab like her mom, and a presence like her father. She was very compassionate and perhaps a workaholic. A beauty, with an entrepreneurial spirit and a true passion and desire to build something great, she pushed herself to achieve her goals. Always positive, she never let anything stand in her way. Amber believed in herself and loved her family. She could be a bit overbearing at times–likely a side effect of mingling with Hollywood's rich, famous, and sometimes superficial crowd. She had a heart of gold, and that reminded Noah that he needed to make a call.

"I'd like to speak to Ted, please—tell him it's Noah."

"Hello, Noah. Ted here. What's up?"

"Hey, Ted, sorry to bother you, but I need to make something happen, and I haven't heard from you. I was wondering if you would find a fifteen percent finder's fee more agreeable? Would that spur you to find us a better deal?"

"Well, yes, Noah. Normally, that would be good, but how much do you have?"

"Ted, honestly—I don't know. I think it's a lot."

"Well, if you have a lot, it will mean a lot to me. So yes, that will be fine. I will renew my efforts," Ted said.

"Thank you, Ted. That's what I was hoping for. Please try."

Now, there was nothing to do but wait—something Noah was notoriously bad at. He needed to be doing something all the time. He found Little Joe by the pool and joined him for an iced tea.

"How are you feeling, sir?" he asked.

"Oh, I'm fine, Noah."

"No, really, sir, how are you doing? After all you have been through, I would be a mess inside. But I seem more upset over what happened than you."

"Well, I don't like showing my feelings. Maybe I'm just trying to stay calm, so I don't worry the ladies. Probably a little of both. It's been hard on me, Noah. I don't enjoy this. What

I can remember, mixed with what I have been told, just leaves me confused. I just don't understand why things played out the way they did. I'm a bit anxious about talking–things still aren't clear to me."

"That's perfectly understandable, sir. It's going to take time. It would worry me if you did not have reservations. I just want you to know that–I don't think you could've done anything differently. I told your daughters that you demonstrated great courage. That much I know for sure." You've got nothing to be ashamed of."

"Thank you, Noah. I really appreciate your thoughtfulness. What concerns me most is going back into that room. It has me worried. It used to be my source for creativity. Can it be again? I shudder to think."

"One thing I'm sure of, sir–if anyone can face their fears, it's you."

Chapter 14

Cause and Effect

Little Joe awoke to the sound of ocean waves pounding the shore. The screeching of seagulls feeding as a gentle breeze moved the white lace curtains that covered his raised bedroom window. He lay motionless on his back, eyes open, arms folded across his chest, listening intently to the sounds of morning in Charleston. Focusing on each distinct sound and testing his senses, he mentally pictured the movements that created each, their cause, and effect. Then his mind let the sounds merge again into a natural symphony. As a writer, it's important to understand sounds and how they are produced. How else can a wordsmith describe them and bring them to life on the pages of a book?

A morning ritual was to say a prayer of thanks for another day on earth. He prayed for each member of his family, his friends, and anyone having problems. He thanked God for all the blessings he had received and prayed for forgiveness, patience, understanding, and the creativity to write words that would lift others. That morning, he also prayed for Michael Bon's soul and for Lydia Bon's recovery.

Then, he considered the day ahead. His first doctor's appointment since leaving the hospital was that morning. He contemplated what he might learn. He pondered going back into his own office. For some reason, he felt anxious about returning to the crime scene. He wondered if it would bring back any suppressed memories that his amnesia had removed. He wouldn't return to that room until he was ready. There was no need to rush.

As was his custom, he remained still and introspective while performing a short self-hypnosis, silently speaking to himself. I control my mind; my mind controls my body. He repeated this several times and began counting from ten backwards down to one, with messages in between. My eyelids are heavy. I'm going deeper and deeper into hypnotic relaxation. Rest, relax. Rest, relax. Deeper and deeper, more and more relaxed with each count. More and more relaxed with each second that passes. When the count reaches zero, I will fall into a state of total relaxation.

Once satisfied that he had delved deep enough into the subconscious mind, he began giving it orders.

"I command my brain to send healing energy throughout my body—to heal and rejuvenate every part of me. I command my mind to give me patience, clarity, imagination, and drive. Today. I will be honest and sensitive to the needs of others. I will have a total recall of all the knowledge I have ever possessed. Today is the first day of the rest of my life, I will be happy and dwell in it."

Feeling the urge to use the bathroom, he ended his self-help program, rolled onto his left side, and lifted himself off his back, finding the floor with his feet. He paused to make sure his old back pain and the bullet wound wouldn't hinder him, then he slowly made his way to the bathroom.

Diane arose at the same time, almost in unison. They walked to the door. She allowed Little Joe to go ahead of her because of his condition; then, she made her way to the kitchen to make coffee.

When Little Joe joined her, they took their coffee out onto the patio to enjoy the cool morning breeze.

"Your doctor appointment is this morning, isn't it?" Diane asked.

"Yes, at nine a.m. I will get cleaned up in a bit and leave early."

"I'll get ready and drive you."

"Okay, that job's all yours," he said.

Noah and Aileen joined them, and they all exchanged greetings.

"How did you sleep last night, sir?" Noah asked.

"Pretty good," Little Joe answered. "Not as much pain this morning from that bullet. I'm on the mend."

"That's good news, Dad," Aileen said. "I was going to ask you if it hurt."

"It did. And well, it does still, but not so bad. It feels much better."

"That's great," Noah said.

"I have a doctor's appointment this morning. Maybe I will learn something about my condition," Little Joe said.

"Have you had any memories return, hon?" Diane asked.

"A little, but it seems unreal. Like it happened to someone else, and I am just reading about it," Little Joe answered. "It's very strange."

"We'll need to tell your doctor about that," Diane said.

"Yes, I will. We had better get ready. I don't want to be late. Noah, you and Aileen can hold down the fort while we are gone. Make sure you get plenty of pool time. I know how much you two like swimming."

"Yes, sir, I will follow your orders and enjoy every minute of it," Noah laughed.

"Okay, I'll see you when we get back," Diane said.

When they arrived at the office complex, the receptionist took Little Joe into a room and directed him to put on a gown. Diane helped him when he could not find the ties.

"These darn things—I can never figure them out," Little Joe muttered.

The doctor was not long. He asked Little Joe a lot of questions that would test his memory. He tested his reflexes, just like he had in the hospital. All of the testing seemed to go well.

Little Joe told him about some memories coming back. The doctor asked for details. Little Joe said he thought he remembered the man entering his office, but that was it. It seemed like something he had seen on television, like it might have happened to someone else. He could not even be sure it was his memory.

The doctor asked him to get dressed, and when he came back, he began explaining Little Joe's condition to him. When he was done, Little Joe and Diane asked a lot of questions. Diane was happy the doctor took his time with them and didn't hurry. They continued the discussion all the way home, each trying to remember everything the doctor said.

Back home, they changed into their swimsuits and joined the others by the pool. Noah asked what the doctor had to say.

"Amnesia isn't easy to understand," Little Joe said.

"In retrograde amnesia, which is what they think I have, the mind loses its ability to recall portions of memory. The memory isn't a recording of an image. It's actually a recording of what happened, so we can replay it. Our brain sees a sheepdog run toward a toy and flip over it hilariously. Our brain records this pattern and sets it to the side, to re-fire those neurons and recreate the event as we see fit. It's also why it's so darn *easy* to reprogram memories. That's a pretty bad explanation, I know, but it's the best I can do."

"Retrograde amnesia can be either a loss of our recordings of the pattern, a failure to recreate the pattern, or our mind's refusal to do it."

"As it was explained to me, in the event of psychological trauma, our mind literally blocks out the re-patterning function as a defense mechanism. Therefore, we no longer remember that we actually *were* nude in class, and it *wasn't* a dream."

"As for trauma, the pattern's recording could be damaged, or the ability to specifically relive that pattern could be damaged. This is how my specialist explained it to me."

"As far as recalling memories forgotten this way, it's tricky. Usually, this happens without treatment in the case of physical trauma. Memories almost never come back all at once."

"So, if someone had retrograde amnesia due to physical trauma, is it still possible to regain their previous memories?" Noah asked.

"The doctor said it's possible," Little Joe said. "But, it depends on the extent of damage, and the memory may not seem real."

"Wow. You learned all that from one doctor visit?"

"Yep, we asked a lot of questions. The thing is, as I understand it, even when I do remember, it may seem unreal. That's okay since the memory would not be a good one anyhow."

"Well, there is something I have to ask. I, well, we-Aileen and I-are very much involved in the events leading up to this problem. And, well, we are curious to know if you remember the gold? And where it is hidden?"

"Ha, ha, ha, ha, you have every right to be questioning. After all, I involved you and nearly got you shot. Yes! I remember it and exactly where it is hidden. Any other memory tests today?"

"Yes!" Aileen bellowed. "You can tell us where it is. And while you're at it, you can tell me why I'm just learning of this. How long are you going to keep this to yourself?"

"Ha, ha, ha, ha, I knew that was coming! I don't blame you for asking. I want to tell you, but I want your sister here when I do. It's only right to tell everyone at one time."

"But she doesn't know anything about it, and might not come home until Christmas!" Aileen said.

"I don't think you'll have to wait that long. I'm expecting her tomorrow," Little Joe responded, grinning all the while.

"She is! When did she tell you that?" Aileen questioned.

"I called her the other day and asked her to come for a visit. I told her I had important news, but she had to come here to hear it," Little Joe said.

"That's good, Dad, I can't wait."

The Storm from the West

The morning sun peered over a dark and eerie Atlantic Ocean. Storm clouds hovered ominously. Though the air remained calm, signs of looming trouble hung on the horizon.

Little Joe welcomed the change from the steady diet of sunshine. Life is meant to be about invigorating experiences, and this looked to be very stimulating indeed. Diane listened to the National Weather Forecast on her iPhone while Aileen tracked the storm on her MyRadar app.

Noah asked Little Joe, "Should we put plywood up over the windows or anything?"

"No," Little Joe replied, "It's never as bad as they say. The winds usually carry the storms around us, but could you call the airport and make sure Amber's flight has not been canceled? She should be coming in at 11:45 if there's no change."

"Sure will, sir," he replied.

The smell of pork chops, eggs, and biscuits from the kitchen signaled that Addie was whipping up something delicious. The aroma proved distracting for the empty stomachs trying to concentrate on a possible storm.

"Man, does that smell good," Noah said while calling the airport.

"Yeah," Little Joe agreed. "I think I'll sneak in and snag one of those biscuits while I wait. It's pretty good cooking that can compete with a possible category 2 hurricane."

"If you grab two, I'll be happy to take one off your hands." Noah joked as his father-in-law left the room.

"I'll see what I can do." On returning from the kitchen, Little Joe said, "Addie is on to my tricks; she's hiding her biscuits in the warmer." He laughed. "I don't think she trusts me."

"Bummer," Noah said. Hanging up the house phone, he turned and told Little Joe, "The airport is open and all planes are on time for now. We'll have to check back in an hour or so. Don't let me forget to do that."

Addie left her kitchen unguarded long enough to tell Diane she would set a table in the dining room if that was okay. Diane, still listening to the weather, nodded in agreement.

The ample windows that generally allowed plenty of morning sunlight now contributed only a gloomy, grayish environment. Diane, taking notice, turned the lights on in the hallway and dining room.

"That's better," she said. "No sense sitting in the dark."

Soon after they were seated, Addie first placed a pot of coffee on the table, then positioned a platter of biscuits, a large bowl of gravy, and a dish of eggs on the tabletop. The smiling faces around the table were proof of Addie's skill in the kitchen. Little Joe asked her to sit with them and enjoy her breakfast, but she declined, saying she had work to do. He asked if she was worried about the storm.

"Don't reckon it'd do me no good to worry. The good Lord will see us through."

"Well, if you would like to go home early today, feel free to do so. We appreciate you coming out this morning."

"I thank you, Mr. Joe. I'll think on it."

"Well, you know you're welcome to ride out the storm here with us if you want, but if you would feel better at home, that's okay too."

"I reckon I'll go home after I get some things done here. Might be some nerves that need calming there."

"You do as you please, Addie, and be sure to tell your husband 'hi' for us when you go home. We sure envy him for having your cooking for so many years; he's a lucky man."

"I'll do that, Mr. Joe. Wouldn't hurt to remind that old lazy man how good he has it."

Little Joe laughed as he spooned thick, peppery pork chop gravy over his biscuits. "Man, I love this stuff!" he said. "Just like Momma used to make. I'll have to go back to the gym if I keep eating like this."

"You and me both," Noah chimed in.

"You might as well enjoy it while you can because when Amber gets here, she'll have us all drinking protein shakes with kale and spinach," Aileen said.

Diane laughed with everyone else. "You better believe that! She'll be on our backs, telling us how to make our skin glow," she said.

"I know this gravy is not good for me, but I can't help but glow when I'm eating it. I don't know what my skin is doing, but I'm happy all over. It's probably a good thing she is coming. It won't hurt to eat better for a little while. It won't hurt any of us. But what are we going to tell Addie when

Amber starts telling her how to make tofu salads?" Little Joe said, laughing.

"Amber really knows her stuff when it comes to staying thin and looking healthy. You gotta hand it to her on that. I suppose all California models are like that," Aileen said.

"Yeah, I could use a little work on my girlish figure," Noah said. "But I should have started about one hundred pounds ago," he said, sliding two more eggs onto his plate.

"Amber and Addie are not going to get along at all!" Diane laughed.

After breakfast, they gathered in the living room for more coffee. Noah called the airport again and received the same response.

"Everything is normal at the airport, sir," he said. "We should probably leave around ten or so, in case there are any road delays. Aileen told Amber last night to call us when she exited the plane, and we will drive slowly around to passenger pickup, looking for her."

"Good idea," Little Joe said.

"I'm going to get ready now. Be back in a bit." Little Joe headed down the hall to his bedroom. He slowed as he passed his office, but didn't stop. His mind harkened back to that night when his memory left him. He half wanted to go in and greet his demons, if he had any, but didn't. Instead, he entered his bedroom, turned on the lights, and began laying out clothes for the day.

Showered and dressed, he once again entered the hallway, heading for the living area. This time, when he neared the door to his beloved *sanctum sanctorum*, he could no longer resist its attraction. Hesitating for a second, he turned the heavy brass handle on the door, opening it slowly. It was like going in for the very first time. It was both comfortable and new to him. He closed the door and turned on the lights. The room felt less intimidating once illuminated. As he looked, he wondered how anything bad could have happened there. Nothing was disturbed or out of place, and no horrible images came to him. Nothing like what he had been told happened. It was just an empty room. If anything happened there, he would have to imagine it because he had no recollection. He was happy about that because the anxiety he experienced had placed doubt in his mind.

Slowly, he moved around the desk to his large leather chair and its position of authority. Lowering himself into the chair and feeling the rich leather surround him, he felt he was the master again of his thoughts, the lord of his domain.

It was important for him to gauge his mental state before Amber arrived. Her personality was strong, and she was not used to following directions. Her eighteen years in Hollywood had made her tough. She made a life and career by sheer will. She rose early each day and beat the streets looking for modeling and acting jobs. According to her, she did well because she didn't drink or do drugs and made finding work a full-time job. It's what she wanted to do, and she would not be denied. This type of single-mindedness in a personality was useful in Hollywood, but not in a family setting. Little Joe knew families worked better when unity could be achieved. Harmony was derived from the attitude of, who can best work and best agree. Working toward shared family goals with like-minded people wasn't a valued trait in Hollywood. He wondered if she would be able to work in harmony with him and the others. Regardless, he would have to tell her about the treasure, and he would have to stay in control. This and more went through his mind as he sat there in that place most conducive to thought.

Knowing he would never hear any calls from Diane, he grudgingly rose and stepped away from the chair. Walking to the door, he felt a tinge of creativity hidden under a shelf of worry and doubt, and he would have liked to linger.

Satisfied he had faced a demon and won, Little Joe returned to the others. Aileen continued tracking the storm on her phone, keeping everyone updated. It was still a category two and had not yet leveled its eye directly at Charleston. It's fifty-mile-per-hour winds were heading in a northern direction and still out at sea. The real storm would arrive soon from Hollywood. And no amount of preparation could reduce its impact.

Chapter 15

The Reunion and the Secret

The heavy rain slashed sideways at times, slowing traffic to a crawl. With Noah driving and Little Joe in the passenger seat, they slowly made their way to Charleston International Airport, north of Charleston. Little Joe quietly prayed the plane would land safely in this torrential downpour. He had not seen Amber in over a year and was anxious to spend some time with her.

She had left home at twenty-one for Hollywood with dreams of stardom—and she had done well. She studied acting at the prestigious Groundlings Academy, performed on soap operas, and had small parts in several movies. She had leading roles in a few music videos and many commercials. She worked a lot at her craft.

Of late, she had begun an online store selling ladies' clothing. That, too, was doing well. She constantly pushed herself and often grew impatient with those who didn't match her energy.

Nearing the airport, Noah pulled to the side to check his phone for messages.

"They have landed early, sir. She is on her way to baggage claim and will meet us at passenger pickup."

"Oh, that's great news. She is safe, and we won't have to wait long," Little Joe said. As they drove down the passenger pickup lane, she was easy to spot. Her long blond hair and bright smile shone brightly through the dull rainy afternoon. She was wearing black tights, a white top with a boa and stiletto heels, and pulling a suitcase almost as big as she was. She looked as out of place in Charleston as he would in Hollywood, he thought.

Little Joe exited the car as quickly as Noah could pull to the curb. His anxiety turned to joy at seeing her again. He hugged her and kissed her cheek, just like he used to when sending her off to school years ago.

"Welcome home, Amber. We missed you."

"I missed you, too, Dad. How is your wound?" she said, studying him.

"I'm fine, hon, getting better every day."

"You scared the heck out of me. I would have been there, you know, but mom knew I was involved in a new project, and she didn't want to upset me. They didn't tell me until you were much better. They said they thought we were going to lose you. Ever find out what that crazy guy was after?"

"Yeah," he said. "I'll tell you all about it later,"

Noah took her suitcase and heaved it into the trunk, as though it were empty. Opening the door for her, he said, "How are you doing, young lady?"

"I'm fine, Noah. What's crackalackin' with you? How's my big sister treating you?"

"She is the joy of my life. Wouldn't know what to do without her."

"You're a lucky guy, Noah."

"I sure am. How have you been?"

"I'm doing great. I've been selected for a new reality show, if it gets picked up."

"What's that all about?"

"I'll tell you all about it later. What's up with this storm? Is it going to get bad down here?" Amber asked.

"Probably not," Little Joe answered. "Mother Nature is just kicking up a fuss to break the monotony of sunshine and the soothing sound of the ocean."

"I can't wait to see your new place. Is it nice, Dad?"

"It is, Amber. I think you will like it."

"Mom seems to like it. She says so when we talk on the phone. Do you like it, Noah?" she said.

"Oh yes, it is so close to the Atlantic, you can watch the sun rise and listen to the waves rushing to the shore every morning. I love it."

The small talk continued for the duration of the drive home. As they pulled up the blacktop driveway, Amber gushed over how pretty the approach was.

"Wow, I can't wait to see inside," she said.

Diane and Aileen were waiting at the door to greet them. Noah let Amber out under the carport to keep her dry, then parked the car safely in the garage. Noah grabbed her suitcase and took it into the kitchen. Little Joe followed behind. The job finished, the two of them made coffee and looked for the cake Addie had made before she left.

Smiles and laughter filled the house as Diane and Aileen gave Amber a full tour. She had seen every part except for one room. Passing back down the hall toward the family room, Amber asked, "What's in this room, Mom?"

Diane touched the brass door handle and, looking at Amber, began to cry. "This is where it happened. Where we almost lost your father."

"Don't cry, Mom." Amber took her hand. "Dad's okay now. I want to see his room."

Opening the door, she admired how stylish the room was. "Wow, did Dad design this room himself?"

"Yes, it's soundproof, and he has all kinds of special lighting and music that he plays. It's where he does his writing. There, bent over that desk, is where Aileen and I found him. We thought he was dead. There was a lot of blood. The other man lay over there. He was dead. Noah was with your father when it happened and tried to help him."

"Oh, Mom, you and Aileen must have been terrified finding him like that. How have you been since that night? Are you okay? Obviously not, you're crying. Let's get out of here and go somewhere you'll be comfortable," Amber suggested.

"I'm okay, it just affects me once in a while, when I think about how close it was. It was awful."

"Everything is going to be okay now, Mom," Aileen said, taking her mom around the shoulder and leading her to the door.

"Is this why Dad sent for me? What's going on?" Amber said, her eyes open wide and her arms extended, palms up.

"Your Dad will tell you. I don't know everything myself. He will tell us all soon."

"Starting to get pretty damn serious around here. Let's have a glass of wine." Amber knew how to liven things up and change the mood. "Let's get this party started."

Back in the kitchen, they found the men enjoying coffee and cake at the table.

"Eating cake in the middle of the day, are you sure you want to do that?" Amber asked, smiling. "What's the plan for burning those calories off?"

"Never gave it a thought, Amber," Little Joe said.

"I know you didn't, Dad, but you have to have a plan if you're going to stay healthy. You won't find any cake in my house."

"That's why I'm here instead of at your house. This cake is so good."

"You're going to be sorry. That cake is going to come back and haunt you when you're trying to look like a stud out there on that beach."

"I'll take that under advisement, hon. I know you're right. But the flesh is weak." Little Joe decided to change the subject. "How do you like the house?"

"It's really nice, Dad. I'm impressed."

"Well, if you're impressed, we must have done a great job. I know how hard you are to please."

Suddenly, a loud crash echoed from outside.

"What was that?" Amber exclaimed.

"Sounds like the wind took hold of our garbage containers outside. I should check on things," Little Joe said.

"I'll get it, sir," Noah said, raising himself from the table.

"This storm is wild," Amber said. "Hope it lets up soon."

***

The storm raged into the night. The girls, having changed into their warmest pajamas, sat on the floor in front of the living room fireplace, telling stories, watching the flames flicker, and reconnecting.

Everyone's heart brimmed with the joy of family. Smiles and laughter parted more lips than the occasional sip of wine. Little Joe thought, *home and hearth, kith and kin, this is what life is all about.*

Noah and Little Joe sat nearby, enjoying the laughter, saying little. It was the girls' moment to enjoy. The men's interloping was tolerated but not encouraged. They didn't mind because it was fun watching the girls reminisce.

Family, Little Joe thought, and precious moments, building memories.

The atmosphere was marred only by an occasional crash of lightning that lit up the room, casting shadows on the walls, and gusts of wind and rain hitting the window. The great oak limbs in the yard swayed back and forth, creaking with the wind, taking a beating, and demanding attention.

"This storm reminds me of a time when we were young, living in Beaver Falls. None of us could sleep because the lightning kept the sky lit up, and the thunder kept booming so loudly all around us. We brought our blankets into the living room. Dad and Mom crawled under them with us on the floor. Every time the lightning crashed, we would all scream. Remember that night, Aileen?"

"Yeah, I remember–Mom and Dad were just as scared as we were."

"I do remember that," Little Joe said, "That was a really bad electrical storm, so we tried to have some fun with it."

"Are you going to tell me why I'm here, Dad?" Amber asked.

"Tomorrow–when the storm has passed and the wine bottle is corked again."

"Aren't you going to have a glass with us?"

"Sure, I'll have one, but no more than that for me, at least until this storm lets up."

Pouring Little Joe a glass of wine, she asked Noah, "Would you like one, too?"

"Sure, sounds good," he said.

"You guys are being pretty quiet. What's going on?"

"We're just listening and taking notes," Noah said. "Figure I can blackmail you ladies someday if I save all these stories you're telling."

"Go ahead–don't make me put a hit on you, Noah," Amber said with a laugh.

"The National Weather Service is predicting heavy flooding in this area, Dad," Aileen said. "I've been watching it on my phone app. Does it flood here?"

"Well, it hasn't yet, but there's always a first time. I think we are too high."

"Oh, my gosh, Dad," Aileen said. "Maybe you'd better check outside. Do we have a boat or anything in case it floods?"

"I really don't think we have to worry about that, but I'm keeping an eye on things just in case. We'll be fine," Little Joe answered.

Feeling a twinge of doubt in his own prediction, he walked to the window and peered outside. The dark of the night and the lights behind him made it impossible to see anything.

"Noah, it's not safe to stand by a window during a storm like this." Little Joe said.

"Come with me. We can open the garage door and get a better look without the glass in front of us."

Noah found the button beside the man-door and pushed it. Opening the garage door allowed the rain to blow sideways across the once-dry floor. An empty plastic trash container flew into the garage and slid to the opposite side, as if by magic. Little Joe jumped back and then grabbed his chest area where he had been shot, feeling a sharp pain. A chill washed over him, and he backed up against the wall.

The storm increased in intensity.

"Close the door, Noah. There's nothing to do but wait and pray. It's too dangerous out there—and we can't see a thing." It's just too bad," Little Joe said. "What do you think?"

"I think you're right, sir. Maybe we should go to your office to wait it out. That's the safest place in the house."

"You might be right, Noah. I never thought it would get this bad. I don't want to scare anyone. Let's wait a little longer and see if there is any change."

"Yeah, it could just as easily let up. I hope so," Noah said.

Back inside, Little Joe headed to his bedroom to grab a sweater. As he passed the living room, Aileen asked if everything was all right. He nodded, giving a thumbs-up. "No problem."

Noah, who was right behind him, walked into the living room where he'd left his phone. He pulled up the National Weather Forecast app so he could monitor it himself.

Diane lifted herself up from the floor. "Anybody hungry? I'm going to see what Addie left for us to eat."

"I'm hungry," Amber said.

"How about you, Noah?" Aileen asked.

"Heck yeah, I'm famished."

Diane found a sandwich ring. It had three types of delicious deli meats layered with toasted red bell peppers, spicy pepper rings, and two layers of cheese. The aroma wafting from the microwave was sure to bring the boys running. Pulling out pickles and other condiments, she set a table. Before long, they all gathered around it.

"You know, that's a lot of bread, folks. You're not winning the calorie battle here," Amber said, as a jab. "But it sure smells good. When am I going to meet this Addie?"

"She'll be here tomorrow morning if this storm doesn't blow us all away," Diane said.

"I can't wait. She sure works magic with flour and water."

Though he didn't want to ruin the family fun, Little Joe was growing more concerned about the storm. Entering the dining room, he asked, "Noah, what is your weather app saying?"

"The storm is definitely worsening, sir. It's showing a lot of red right over top of us."

The Secret

"Why don't we take our food and drinks into my office, where we will be safer," Little Joe said.

"Do you think it's dangerous?" Aileen asked, her face clearly showing anxiety.

"No, I don't, but there is no reason to take any chances. We will be just as comfortable in there, and there will be less to worry about."

"I'll grab the sandwich ring; you girls get the drinks. Let's do as your father suggests," Diane said.

Little Joe's office was quiet compared to the rest of the house, and the mood changed dramatically. Everyone was now focused on the silence and the looming danger. Little Joe wanted to make them feel relaxed, safe, and secure.

Sitting back in his big chair, he asked, "Who's slicing the sandwich ring? I don't usually eat after 7:00 pm, but I'll make an exception tonight."

Everyone settled in. Noah had brought chairs from the dining room, and Diane set the food on Little Joe's desk.

Amber spoke up, "I'll cut you a very small piece, *a moment on the lips, a lifetime on the hips,*" she said. No one laughed. The mood had shifted–gaiety gave way to tension. Little Joe sensed it and felt the time was right to tell them why they were there.

"Family, I believe now's the right time to tell you why I asked you all to come. I hadn't planned on doing this until tomorrow, but there is no reason to wait, and we need something to take our minds off that darn storm, anyhow. I would just like to ask for your patience as I try to explain something. Today is a big day for me. I've carried a heavy secret for a long time–and honestly, I've never liked secrets. Today I want to share it with you, but only if you promise to keep it between us. It is an incredible story."

"I'm on the edge of my seat, Dad, just spit it out," Aileen said.

"*No,* this is not the kind of secret you spit out. This is something I've struggled to keep much of my life, and if I share it with you, you'll have to bear the weight of it too. I'm not sure I'm doing you any favors, but I'm at a time in my life where I can no longer keep it to myself. I almost died, and if that had happened–well, Noah knew part of my secret, but not the whole story. My secret would have died with me. I can't take a chance on that happening again. I need you to listen and understand; it means a great deal to me."

With their undivided attention, he began telling his story. He recounted the capture of Jefferson Davis and the Confederate Treasury. He told them about Tennessee's troops being attacked and how the gold vanished. He spoke of the moonlight marriage, the midnight murder, and the strong, remarkable people whose lives were both blessed and burdened by that gold. He told them how his mother had buried it in mason jars in their backyard garden and how he discovered her letter years after her death. How he dug up the gold–and another message from her–and how his tears fell remembering all who had died. Little Joe explained his decision to keep the gold a secret and not use it for personal gain.

"With Noah's help, we were able to find buyers for the gold, and soon, hopefully–it will be gone forever. Michael Bon had known about the gold. The story had passed from father to son. He nearly killed me. I "regret" his death, but it made finding a resolution more urgent than ever." After sharing the story as best he could, he asked, "Any questions?"

"I have one," Aileen said. "Can I see Grandma's letter– the one you found in the garden?"

"Sure, it's on the mantel above the fireplace, still in the same jar where I found it."

"Dad," Amber said, "I can't believe this. You mean you were sitting on a literal pot of gold and never said one word to any of us? Do you know how many times that money could've helped us?"

"I do know. I have thought about it many times, but I believe it was more important for us to stand on our own–to learn responsibility and find our own path. We all did fine without it, but with it, you might never have developed the qualities I admire in each of you. We're here now, doing just fine, and we can be proud of our accomplishments—because we didn't ask for anything from anyone. We did it on our own."

"I don't know. I think life could have been a lot easier," replied Amber.

"Yes, but anything gained too easily is rarely truly appreciated. If you think about it, I believe you'll come to agree. I did what I believed was best."

Chapter 16

The Art of the Deal

The weeks and months after the reunion passed quickly. Little Joe had long wondered whether the book would be a novel or a novella. His word count was well over 70,000, making it a novel, but there was a lot of editing to be done. Little Joe called upon his old friend, Greg Girvan, to help speed up the process. Greg had previously edited parts of the manuscript and was already familiar with it. Little Joe engaged Susan, a friend of his cousins Richard and Tereasa, in Knoxville, Tennessee, to help with character development. Susan worked for the University of Tennessee and specialized in character development–bringing them to life, and making the storyline pop.

This was the process that went into developing a manuscript for publication. Writing a book can take years, and editing often takes months, but for Little Joe, the writing went much faster because he had been carrying the entire story around in his head for years. That, along with the help from his Writers Guild friends, was finally coming together, and he was very excited.

"Honey, is my laundry back from Low Country Dry Cleaners?" asked Little Joe.

"Yes, they delivered it this morning. Your white shirts are in the dresser drawer."

"Thank you."

"Where are you going?"

"I'm heading over to meet Greg."

"You are going full steam ahead on this, aren't you? I thought we were going to talk about releasing it or not."

"Honey, you know how much I love this book. And you know I would never do anything to hurt this family."

"Yes, I know you would never do anything *on purpose* to hurt us, but have you considered everything that could go wrong? Have you examined every possibility?"

"I think I have. Has Addie arrived yet? I don't want to be overheard. Come here for a moment; let's talk in my office."

Closing the door behind them, Little Joe flipped the light switch on and moved to his desk. Sitting on its corner, he looked down, then up directly at Diane. "Look, I can't say there will not be any blowback. And it might be uncomfortable again, like it was before. But if you trust me, we can weather any storm."

"I do trust you, Joe, but it's not just us, you know. It could be hard on the girls, too, and Noah. And what if you are charged with something? I almost lost you once. I don't want to risk losing you again."

"Of those to whom much is given, much is expected. That may not be a direct quote, and I'm not sure who said it, but it fits. We have been given much. And you know what, after the way the newspapers and lawyers treated us, I half hope they do want to start something."

"Oh, please don't say that! I've never seen you go into anything blind, and you sure as hell better not this time. That's all I have to say."

"That's not all you are going to say. "And you said you trust me. You do, right?"

"Of course, I trust you, and I'll stand with you, no matter what. The kids can move back to Pittsburgh if they can't take it," Diane said. "What is this book, Joe?" she asked, pointing to a large, dark, heavy-looking hardback on his desk.

"Oh, I borrowed some books from the library. You know I studied law for one year. I like to read up on the subject every now and again."

"I don't know when you would find the time for a volume that big. Well, alright. Do as you please with your book. I'll stand by you, no matter what," Diane said, leaving the room.

Little Joe made some phone calls and learned that Greg and Susan had finished their work on the manuscript.

He had his agent shop the book around to several publishing houses to see who might be interested in it. Several expressed interest, but only one, Fleischman Publishing, impressed Little Joe with their ability to market his book.

"How many do you think you can sell?" Little Joe asked Fleischman.

"Maybe thirty thousand copies."

"Would you be satisfied with that number?" Little Joe asked.

"I think so," replied the publisher.

"Well, if the sales go up to 75,000, that will please you even more, correct?"

"Yes, but I must advise you, I think you are being overly optimistic!"

"Well, now, if you priced me at the potential for 30,000 sales, I want 10 % more of the profits on every book sold over that number. That should be acceptable since you don't expect that to happen."

"Mr. McKirdy, I have been in the publishing business a very long time, and I don't recommend being overly optimistic."

"Does that mean you agree? If so, I only have one more question before you draw up the new contract."

"Of course, I will be happy to put that in the agreement. What else is on your mind?"

"Can you print that many books without delay?"

"Yes, we can produce that and more, I assure you."

"Good, put that in the contract as well. Send it to my office, and I will sign it."

As Little Joe cruised toward home in their new Lincoln Continental, he tried out the XM radio. The controls on the left side of his steering wheel would change stations and raise or lower the volume. Music from the '50s, '60s, and '70s played with a flick of his thumb. He lowered the volume so he could think and wondered if he was doing the right thing. How bad could it get? It was not too late to change his mind. He had one more day. Tomorrow, he would either sign the contract or tear it up.

Diane had planned a poolside gathering for the family. They would all be there tonight. He wondered if they would support him or be angry. He braced himself for the worst.

When his children began to arrive, they found Little Joe quietly staring out at the ocean. One by one, they came through the French doors onto the patio. But Little Joe did not notice. He did not turn but sat seemingly transfixed, as though a 'do not disturb' sign hung from him. No one spoke. They knew they were witness to something rare, maybe a personal moment, though they didn't know what it was. They waited in silence for the answer.

Realizing he was no longer alone, Little Joe turned to his family.

"You looked like you were meditating or something. We hated to disturb you," Noah said.

"When I find a quiet time, and conditions are perfect, I meditate and consult my invisible counselors," Little Joe replied.

"What are your invisible counselors, Dad?" Aileen asked.

"You never told your daughters, sir? Shame on you," Noah quipped.

"No time for that now. I'm starved. Does Addie know we are all here, Diane?"

"Yes, she's getting things ready."

The Family Gold

After dinner, Little Joe asked everyone to pray with him.

"I have a lot on my plate right now, family. I want to always do the right thing, but sometimes, it's not possible. I'm torn, I'm conflicted, and I need help."

"What is it, Dad?" Amber asked.

"This family has lived under a cloud since 1898, that's 120 years, and I think that's long enough: my lifetime, my parents' lifetime, my mom's family, and those before them. It's time for the load to be lifted from our shoulders. The gold is gone, and I have to thank you, Noah, for helping me get it done. It was a burden lifted, and there is no proof now that it ever existed."

"This book is the only record, the only proof that this family lived, and the amazing part they played in history. Plain, ordinary folks with no desire in the world to be involved in anything like this. For the most part, the gold was thrust upon them. They were forced to live out their lives guarding a secret of little benefit to them. Haunted by the fear of detection, hounded by the law, and balancing all that with a desire to be nothing more than good Christians. It was a job they took on with uncanny skill. In 120 years, only one man figured them out; now he is gone. They stuck together, and now we need to stick together."

"I want to go forward with the book. It's not the same as confessing the whole business and getting it out into the open because it will be touted as a "historical fiction". And I don't want to be the first in my family to go to jail because of it. But, by putting it out there, I'll feel I've lived up to my promise. The promise I made myself was that I would someday honor my mother and father and my ancestors. This book will be my monument to them. I've used all their names in a way that if they could read it, they would know themselves. The historical portion of the book is very accurate. Every member of my extended family, my cousins and their families, will be able to recognize their family and better understand their rich history. It will be a treasure, not of gold, but in terms of a keepsake. To its readers, the gold will just be a part of the expected dramatic license. I don't expect any suspicion to befall us. But if it does, I'll be ready. *We* will be ready for it! Are you with me?""

Amber was the first to speak up, lending her support. "Anything I can do to help, Dad, I'm with you!"

"Noah and I are with you too, Dad," Aileen said. We know how much it means to you, and we support you. We want to be on your book launch team."

"Yes, sir. We're here to help," Noah added.

"What about you, Diane?" Little Joe asked.

"It's been a long road. I'm certainly not going to let you go it alone now," she said.

"Great! I have jobs for everyone. Your support means the world to me. Tomorrow, I will sign a contract with Fleischman Publishing."

***

It was nearly noon the next day before the contract arrived via email. Little Joe printed it out and began reading the dry, uninteresting pages. Finding everything in order, he signed the document, then sent it to his lawyer to have him double-check for errors.

Along with the contract, Little Joe sent instructions for his lawyer to send the contract back to Fleischman Publishing when he was finished.

After lunch, Little Joe gathered some papers and placed them in his briefcase.

"Are you going out, Joe?" Diane asked.

"Yes, I need to visit Greg Girvan again. I have another job for him."

"Another book?"

"No, I need him to do some other things for me. I have to take those law books back to the library, too. I won't be long. Do you need anything while I am out?"

"No, I'll be working on my genealogy. I had some Polish language documents interpreted, and I need to get them organized."

"Okay, I'll see you a little later," Little Joe said, leaving the house.

Upon his return, Little Joe quickly disappeared into his office. Diane, curious about his many errands of late, followed him.

"What are you up to, Joe?" she said.

"I'm trying to tie up any loose ends," Little Joe said. "I don't like leaving anything to chance. I have a question for you, Diane. I know you are busy, but could you find time to head up my book launch team? I need someone good to manage the members. Someone with organization skills as well as tact. I can't think of anyone who would be better suited for the job than you."

"How can I turn down a compliment like that? How many do you have on your launch team?"

"Only six right now. The girls, Noah, you, and a couple from my writer's guild volunteered."

"How many do you need?"

"I hope to have at least twenty."

"Do you have a plan?"

"I have a rough one right now. We can finish it in a few days together. I need at least twenty people to read the book and write a review. Once released, each will purchase it and leave a review. Then they can encourage their followers on Facebook, Twitter, etcetera, to purchase the book as well, and leave a review. Receiving numerous good reviews will help the book get more visibility online. There's more, but it is not hard and will be a great help."

The wheels were set in motion. The book was a reality, and there was no turning back. Little Joe sought every avenue to promote his book. Numerous newspaper and radio ads touted the story of family and gold.

Little Joe's book launch team came together and began the slow, methodical process of marketing his book. Working in conjunction with the publisher, they reached all their goals. The book quickly gained traction on social media and attracted attention throughout the region.

He organized many book signings locally. He reflected on the parallels between the storyline and real events, relieved that few asked pointed questions about the shooting

***

Meanwhile, Lydia Bon was on the mend after her surgery. But while her former husband's death was a shock to her, she was not well at the time and not able to follow the newspaper stories. She did not remember much of her questioning by the police. When she learned that Michael had named her as his sole beneficiary, the first thing she did was visit the home they once shared. There, the memories of him and that place came flooding back. Along with them came questions she couldn't answer. Why was Michael in Charleston, South Carolina? Why did he die there? What possessed him to travel all that way? As she read through the pile of newspapers that accumulated during her recovery, she was surprised to recognize the name of an author in Charleston, the man who shot Michael. She remembered Michael having mentioned that name. She wondered, too, why the police did not mention their connection. Why would they assume that Michael was a midnight robber when he had never broken the law before? It didn't make sense.

Learning that Little Joe had written a book, she purchased a copy, hoping to gain some insight into the man who seemed so mysterious to her.

Discussing the case with the local police force in Johnson City did not satisfy her curiosity, so she decided to visit the lead detective in the case, Officer David Granati.

On the bus trip to Charleston, South Carolina, she went over her concerns until she became certain in her own mind that it had not been investigated properly.

Lydia was 5'8" and carried twenty extra pounds from inactivity while healing from her surgery. Her brown eyes were gentle yet striking. Her once-black, now-gray hair was pulled back neatly into a bun. She walked ably and deliberately. A mole on her chin was the only facial feature misplaced.

Finding Detective Granati in his office, Lydia told him her story and concerns. She began by telling him about her surgery and how it saved her life.

"That's wonderful news, but how does that involve the Charleston Police Department?" he asked.

"Well, the thing is, I could not afford my surgery. It was paid for by an unknown benefactor. I have been unable to learn who it was, so I could thank them. Also, the surgery was pretty involved and kept me laid up for a while. When questioned by the Johnson City police about Michael's death, I was not in a mentally stable condition."

"I can understand your desire to find this mysterious gift giver, but these things do happen, Mrs. Bon."

"Yes, but you see, I inherited the Michael Bon estate, he being my late husband and all. And well, Detective Granati, I happen to know that Michael had a long-time obsession with the man who shot him. That never came out, and I can't imagine why."

"What type of obsession? Can you be more specific?"

"Not very specific, but he had an unusual hatred for a man he had never met."

"Mrs. Bon, I need you to be more detailed as to how all this involves me."

"Well, Officer, you were the lead detective in the case, and you determined that it was a simple case of self-defense. But Michael had no record of ever being involved in any criminal activity. So why would he drive 325 miles to rob a man he had never met and had no connection to?"

"Ma'am, I need evidence or witnesses to file a murder charge, and I had neither. Do you have any evidence at this time that would make a difference?"

"Yes, I think I do. I have the knowledge that the two men knew each other in some way. Michael Bon hated him. And the Michael Bon I knew lived his entire life in near poverty, but for some reason always expected to be rich. How he intended to do that, I have no idea. But he believed it, with all his heart."

"Ma'am, that is all very interesting, and I promise I will add these details to the case record, but I do not, at this time, believe it is enough to open a murder case."

"Well, there is one more thing that might change your mind."

"What is that, Mrs. Bon?"

"Mr. McKirdy's new book is titled *The Family Gold.*' Have you read it?"

"No, I don't have much time for reading."

"I brought you a copy. You will find it very interesting. I believe it ties everything together nicely. Also, my Michael kept a tin box in his attic with many keepsakes. It is missing, and since the police are the only ones who have been in his house since his death, well, it is suspicious, to say the least."

"I'll take a look at this, but I can't promise anything. Thank you for stopping in to see me and sharing your thoughts. I'll be in touch if I have any further questions."

Lydia interjected as she turned to leave. "Gold is always a good motive for murder–and a compelling reason to drive 320 miles."

"Oh, and I contacted the local television station. I think they are interested in revisiting this case from a new angle. If Michael crossed state lines to commit a crime, isn't that a federal case? One more thing, officer, can you think of anyone more capable of paying my doctor's bills, or one with a better reason?"

The look on his face told her that he fully understood her not-so-subtle message.

After she left, he pulled the case file and scribbled some notes on a paper to be included. Her mention of the television news piqued his curiosity and raised his ire He knew they would like nothing better than to stir things up. He would need to be prepared. The seeds of suspicion had been planted, and instead of putting the file back where he found it, he placed it in his briefcase to take home. He had a good record, but one stain could ruin it.

Chapter 17

The Tattled Tale

Before Detective Granati could leave work that day, reporters from the Charleston Sun Times were at his door. Suddenly, a case that had long been closed was making front-page news again. Not what he wanted. The questions were pointed and demanded answers he had not prepared for.

Did the police know that Joseph McKirdy was known by the man he shot to death in his home?

Did the police know about his relationship to the missing $500 million in Confederate Gold?

Did they connect the shooting death of Michael Bon to his descendant, Jack Bon, who was murdered in Johnson City, Tennessee, in 1898? Or his possible connections to the lost Confederate Treasury?

Did they know this was the only connection between them, and that McKirdy actually wrote about that connection?

The stories would be written about one of the most enduring mysteries of the war, the lost Confederate Treasury, now possibly valued as high as $500 million. A story so titillating that it has never gone away. The lure of gold has kept the story alive all these years, and treasure hunters are still actively searching for it.

This was more than enough to give the story front-page status.

The morning paper read like a London tabloid.

The Post and Courier

Winner of the Pulitzer Prize

Headline: Murder mystery shrouded in legends of Gold.

Byline: Is Charleston home to Confederate Gold Millions?

"A new book has hit the bookshelves with a mystery 120 years old. Confederate gold that would be worth many millions in today's money. Two murders, 120 years apart, same names, same family, same reason: gold. Who done it? This is the question raised by the prime suspect, local writer–author Joseph McKirdy. The book, "The Family Gold," was released on February 10th, 2020, through Fleischman Publishing. It can be found on amazon.com/books.

The story begins in 1898 with one of Joseph McKirdy's ancestors. His name, Tennessee Adams, once a member of the Tennessee Cavalry and the Union Army, describes how his unit was tasked with capturing President Jefferson Davis, the fleeing President of the Confederacy, along with the entire Confederate Treasury. After they overtook Davis and those with him, his troop was ordered to convey the gold by wagon to Washington, DC. In the process, they were attacked by remnants of both armies who were returning home from the war and had heard about the gold. Outnumbered and unable to defend the gold, many decided not to fight but did share the gold with the attackers. None of the treasure was ever recovered.

Asked for a comment, McKirdy said simply, "It is a work of fiction. I used some historical information to give it realism, but it is a complete work of fiction. You should not read anything into it."

"However, after talking to Lydia Bon, Michael Bon's widow, we learned that he was also shot to death on a moonlit night, in the home of a local author, Joseph McKirdy. McKirdy said it was a robbery gone wrong. But as it turns out, Michael Bon was also the great-great-grandson of Jack Bon, a Pinkerton detective hired to track down the missing Confederate Treasury, and who was also slain after attending a moonlight marriage with ancestors of Joseph McKirdy. It all sounds very mysterious and suspicious, but I guess that's what sells books, and if so, this one should sell well."

***

Asked by this reporter if there were any grounds for reopening the case, lead Detective David Granati said:

"No, the case is closed. A simple case of self-defense. Mr. McKirdy had been shot by the intruder and is still recuperating. We don't have any evidence that would support anything else."

"Is there a connection? Does the Confederate gold still exist? Is it right here in Charleston? I guess we'll have to read the book!"

Reporter: Scott Tady

The **Charleston City Paper** came out the next day with:

"When is a coincidence not a coincidence?"

Was local author Joseph McKirdy defending himself when he shot and killed a Johnson City, Tennessee resident at the author's home in Charleston? The case is closed, Detective David Granati said, but the widow of the deceased thinks differently. "I think he should be charged with murder," she stated. Asked why, she responded, "It is an impossible coincidence."

The story went on to describe how Michael Bon died in Little Joe's home and how there were quite a few similarities between his death and his great, great, grandfather's death 120 years ago.

***

The story was picked up by four other Charleston newspapers, including *The Charleston Chronicle, The Moultrie News, The James Island Messenger*, and *The Daniel Island News*. But when *USA Today*, located in Charleston, South Carolina, picked up the story, it went national.

Little Joe's family gathered close to him while the storm raged all around them. Local television vans amassed outside the new fence that surrounded his home. Major networks called for interviews. Little Joe took it all in stride, but the others were noticeably concerned.

"How do you do it, Dad?" Amber asked. "Aren't you worried?"

"Well, yes, I am worried, but this is not a time to show it. If those sharks smell blood in the water, they will attack viciously. You can't let them see you sweat. If we don't talk to them or act like we are hiding something, they will go away."

"I wish they would go somewhere," Amber said. "I'm sick of them. Aren't you glad I bought you that fence? You just had it put up in time. Those reporters would be up in our yard if it weren't there."

"I am glad we got that up. Keeps them back," Little Joe said.

"Dad, since the **USA Today** ran their story, they're talking about you nationally. I've seen you mentioned on the late shows. Is there any chance you could get into trouble?"

"No, I don't think so. I wouldn't worry if I were you. All this will settle down in a little while."

The words had barely left his lips when the phone rang.

"I'll get it, Dad. It's probably another newspaper," Amber said. After answering the telephone, she said to her dad, "It's the police! They want to talk to you, Dad."

"Hello."

"Hi, Mr. McKirdy, this is Detective Granati. I would like to stop by and ask you a few questions, if you don't mind."

"Sure, Detective, I'm not going anywhere. Any time you want."

"I'll be there in an hour or so."

"No problem," Little Joe said before hearing the phone click off.

"Better make a pot of coffee, honey. Looks like we are going to have company."

"Are you kidding me?" Diane said.

"No. Detective Granati will be stopping by to ask some questions".

"Oh my gosh, I don't think I can take much more of this," she said. "When is it going to end?"

"Not to worry, darling. Just leave us alone when he gets here, if you would, unless he has questions for you, too," Little Joe said.

"In fact, it might be better if all of you stayed out of the way. I will talk to him, answer his questions, and he will leave. Nothing to worry about. We haven't broken any laws."

"I don't want to talk to him if I don't have to," Diane said. "Noah, you, Aileen, and Amber can come with me when he gets here. We will go out by the pool and stay out of their way."

It was not long before the doorbell rang, and Little Joe answered the door.

Detective Granati was slight of build but muscular. His longish black hair had been blown about by the wind, and he brushed it away from his eyes as the door opened. He had a tan face and steely eyes, but a smile that easily broke the ice.

"Come on in, Detective, and tell me what I can do for you."

"Thank you, Mr. McKirdy."

"Call me Joe."

"I had some coffee brought to my office. Follow me and we'll make you comfortable."

"Thank you, I will."

Entering Little Joe's office, the memory of that evening flashed back into the detective's mind. The crime scene was now nice and tidy. His memory quickly placed where the body lay that night, and all the intensity of that evening was briefly relived.

"Have a seat here. Coffee?"

After playing the good host, Little Joe asked the detective, "How can I be of help?"

"First off, I'm glad to see you are doing so well. The last time I saw you here, you were lying across that desk. We thought you were dead."

"Funny thing, officer, I don't have much memory of that evening. They say it may come back, but it's still kind of a blank to me."

"Well, as you can see from the news people surrounding your home, I have no choice but to ask you some more questions about that evening. You say your memory has not returned. How is your health otherwise after taking a bullet?"

"Yes, it is much better, but still I do not have a clear memory of the events of that evening, I'm sorry to say."

"Mr. McKirdy, did you know the man who shot you in this room before that night?"

"No, sir, I did not."

"Did you know the man was a distant relative of a Pinkerton Detective who was murdered, according to your book, 120 years ago?"

"No, I did not know that until later, and there is some doubt that they were related."

"Why do you say that?"

"He may have been, but I don't have any proof."

"Why did you say they were in your book?" Detective Granati asked.

"Officer, a good book can't just say this might have happened. A story has to be told so that it holds the plot together."

"Mr. McKirdy, you wrote that the Pinkerton detective in your book was searching for those who took the Confederate treasure, and that Tennessee Adams was one of those men.

Was he an ancestor of yours? Did he, in fact, have that gold, and did he pass along that gold through generations to you?"

"Officer, you can search me, you can search this whole house, you will not find any gold. I have worked for everything I have, and I dare anybody to say differently," Little Joe said.

"Was the Michael Bon who died here in this room, in fact, blackmailing you?"

"No, sir."

"The theory is that Bon knew you had the gold and attempted to blackmail you. Now you say this isn't true, but in your book, you lay out exactly that scenario."

"Makes for a good story, doesn't it?" Little Joe quipped. "Officer, I wrote a book. It is clearly labeled as historical fiction because that is what it is. A fictional book must have elements of truth to make it seem true. However, there is also an element of fantasy. Every author uses a degree of dramatic license. You can't say that fantasy is factual because it *seems* to be true. It is supposed to be believable. Otherwise, no one would read it. I can't help it if people want to believe it. Look in my backyard! There have been people out there digging holes looking for Confederate gold coins. They think it is there where my old vegetable garden was. Once they get the fever, there is no stopping them. They will never believe differently. In fact, while you are here, I want to file a report of trespassing and vandalism. Maybe that will stop them from doing it again."

"Mr. McKirdy, there are people who want me to reopen this case. But in all honesty, I don't have any evidence that would justify reopening it. But understand this: it was you who raised doubt in people's minds. The newspapers will fade away before long. But there are a lot of crazies out there. If I were you, I would increase my security. As far as filing a vandalism report, that's not my department. I'll send an officer over to talk with you about that. Good day, sir."

"I'll take that into consideration. Good afternoon, Detective."

"As he passed through the gate at the end of the driveway, Detective Granati was met with shouts. "Will you reopen the case?" "Did you ask about the gold?" "Will there be a murder trial?" All met with a resounding, "No comment!"

Later in the day, a CPD patrolman showed up to write a report of vandalism and trespassing.

As Little Joe explained it, the culprits must have come in the night, armed with picks and shovels. They had dug fourteen holes randomly around the old garden. Each hole is approximately two feet deep. He was clear that he thought the trespassers were looking for buried treasure. To be precise, they were hunting gold coins with CSA (Confederate States of America) on them, jars of gold they thought might be buried there. "They are treasure hunters and not encumbered by little things like laws," Little Joe said.

The officer said little but listened intently as he filled out the report. Before leaving, he turned to Little Joe and asked,

"Mr. McKirdy, the newspapers will get a copy of this report. They're going to eat this story up!"

Little Joe just said, "Thank you, Officer."

***

The newspapers had a field day with the trespass and vandalism report. It summed up what everyone wanted to believe: that the gold existed, and they wanted a clue as to where it was hidden. Their thoughts and suspicions were being woven into fact. To them, the gold was as real as the book. As real as the author's home. And as real as his garden.

The Family Gold even made the front page of *USA Today*, three days in a row, and its readers clamored for more.

The national coverage sent book sales soaring, and it was all Fleischman Publishing could do to keep up with demand.

Little Joe received requests for interviews from the ***Ricky V.*** *talk show in New York City*, the *Late-Night show with **Johnny Cornelius*** in Hollywood, California, and numerous others.

From one end of the country to the other, everyone was talking about **The Family Gold**.

Every talk show and television show host asked the same questions over and over, until Little Joe could answer them in his sleep.

"Mr. McKirdy, everyone wants to know—Is this story true?"

Did your ancestors keep some of the gold from the Confederate Treasury?

Are there millions of dollars in Confederate gold coins buried in your backyard?

It reached the point where he just wanted to shout out the truth, but knew that was not what they wanted to hear. What they wanted was mystery and the lure of riches. He would forever be linked to the crime of another century.

The celebrity status was more than Little Joe could handle. Keeping track of dates and times was becoming a challenge.

"Diane, I don't know if I am supposed to be in Minnesota or Chicago next Tuesday. I thought I wrote it down, but I don't see it in my notes."

"You told me, Chicago–that's what I put on the calendar."

"I'll have to call and make certain," Little Joe said.

Amber, hearing the conversation, suggested her father hire a personal secretary to help him keep track of all his appointments. She suggested a lovely woman she knew.

"Her name is Lenore Ricci, Dad. She's retired and would probably enjoy helping you."

"Give her a call, Amber, and see what she says. I need help."

"Noah, I have to drive up to Johnson City the day after tomorrow for an interview with the **Johnson City Press**, and afterwards, up into the Smokies for a book signing at Dollywood. Would you like to ride along?" Little Joe asked.

"Sure, sounds like a road trip."

"Should be back in four days," Little Joe added.

Noah interrupted: "Sir, you're booked to appear on *Fox and Friends, Fox News,* and five other television programs. You're on page one of almost every newspaper in every city in America. Every television news program is talking about you. Every radio station, even **WXED 107.3 FM** in Ellwood City, is hawking the story. What do you think of that?"

"It is all so surreal. But that's the way it's going to be for a while, I guess. You know, Noah, I would love to just once tell them it's not about me. It's not about murder. It's not even about gold. It's about our family, our ancestors, and my writing. The book is about family.

"You know, some families- aunts and uncles, even brothers and sisters- never speak to one another. Families split over the smallest things. Things they can't even remember. They go all their lives avoiding the only people on earth who have their same story, the same family, and the same DNA."

"If folks take anything away from my book, I want it to be that family should never turn on their own. No matter how much they fight, no matter how much they irritate each other, and no matter how much it hurts at times."

"Remember, when you begin the process of walling yourself off from everyone who upsets your delicate sensitivity, you only end up being alone and miserable. When you limit your pain, you limit your gain."

"Our family fought often. I mean, knock-down drag-out fighting, but we stuck together. We went everywhere together. We laughed, joked, and carried on together. We always knew we were on the same team. That, my friend, was a tradition—an edict, if you will—passed down through at least four generations, as far as I can tell. To love one another, to respect one another, and to defend and support one another. No matter what! Just once, I would like to tell those TV people that, but that's not what they want to hear."

FAMILY IS FOREVER

"Sir, I didn't mean to, but I saw your meeting with the woman who just left. "Was that Lydia Bon? That box she was carrying looked like…"

Without looking up, Little Joe said, "It was."

"She looked remarkably well, and her clothes were stylish and expensive. It's like she must have had a run of good luck since her surgery."

"Yes, Noah, you've found me out. I contacted her. I wanted to explain that evening. I felt she deserved to know what happened, how badly we felt about it, and that it was also not within my power to prevent. No one was to blame. I explained that rather than leave that night as a tragedy in our lives, we should try to make something good come from it."

As he spoke, Diane, Amber, and Aileen entered the room. Aileen, shocked at what she had overheard, cried out, "I can't believe you contacted her after all the terrible things she said about you to the press."

"I didn't really. Actually, I contacted her before she said all those things."

Her eyes widened. "Oh my gosh! You mean to tell me — ?"

"Exactly." Little Joe said, cutting her off.

"You knew she would say all those things?"

"Worse yet, I encouraged it."

"I need to sit down," Noah muttered, slumping into the leather armchair. Lydia Bon went to the police and tried to get them to reopen the case. She brought up your book and all the connections in it. She said it was too much of a coincidence. You knew she would say all that? What would you have done if they had reopened the case?"

"I'm sorry I didn't intend for you to find out this way. I thought I could explain it easily, but now I'm finding it hard."

Diane, realizing her husband had been hiding something from her, raised her hand to her mouth in disbelief. Then, without restraint, she let loose a verbal tirade, demanding he clear the air and tell them exactly what he had done.

"Okay, family–this is going to require some patience and understanding."

"Number one, there was never really a good case against me. It was all hearsay evidence. They wouldn't reopen the case unless they were forced to. All I had to do was wait. With no trial, it became even easier. I simply fed the press what they wanted and they ran with it."

"I had been shamed and embarrassed at having my picture in every paper where I was known. It sullied my good name where I live. The real damage was done, so I allowed the same story to go out to places where I didn't live, to the entire world, and used it to my advantage."

"But why? Why would you go to this extreme?" Aileen asked.

Little Joe turned and retrieved the stained green mason jar from above the fireplace. He opened and lifted the letter it contained from the jar. Holding it near his heart, he said, "My mom suffered to keep this family secret hidden all of her life, and her grandfather and his father, Tennessee Adams, did the same. I can't imagine what they went through to keep this secret and still pass on a legacy of hard work, Christian principles, and an entrepreneurial spirit."

"Also, I told you, I saw in my father a great man. I always loved reading the plaques and monuments honoring war heroes and famous figures—and I wanted to build one to honor him. That began as a small idea in a young man's heart. I thought about it so much I began visualizing this monument in a garden, and my purpose became clear -- a monument to family ideals and a culture of honest, hard work! It became real to me. My book is that monument. It will keep their memories alive–their story alive. And show people how important family is."

"I understand that, Dad," Amber said. "That's not a good reason for deceiving your family and putting us all through a living hell!"

Little Joe took a few seconds to ponder his answer, then spoke in a quiet voice.

"I appreciate what you're saying, Amber, and I feel bad about that. It's like this: my book honors them and promotes family–and I knew the publicity would help get it out there."

Diane, listening intently, let loose another outburst. "Joe, you didn't put us through all this just to sell a book, you couldn't have!"

"You manipulated the press? Where did this idea come from?" Noah asked.

"Actually, Bon gave me the idea. While I was recovering from my bullet wound, it dawned on me how he died for nothing. I felt terrible," Little Joe said, with a tear in his eye. "Then, we learned his whole life had been lived with just one goal in mind. A lonely, sad life to be sure. Why did he die for nothing? I remembered that Napoleon Hill teaches that every failure brings with it the seed of an equivalent success. We must learn to see possibilities, even in our missteps–turn negatives into positives."

"I knew that success comes from making quick, definite decisions, and failure is brought on by indecisiveness and heeding the opinions of others. I didn't want that to happen, so I kept my own counsel, taking no one into my confidence."

"I wouldn't let Michael Bon die for nothing; I used his death to help his former wife and to launch my book. I would've helped him if he'd let me, but he was unhinged–I couldn't reach him."

"It may be hard to understand. But it was a vow I made. And now, I've kept it. I wanted to tell the world what a wonderful family I had, but also how they could have a wonderful family as well, if they would just follow the Golden Rule, work hard, and be determined."

"You know my faith has always been very strong. I was struck by one line of the Bible that always kept popping up, in Matthew 17:20 ESV. It reads, *"For truly, I say to you, if you have faith like a grain of mustard seed, you will say to this mountain, 'Move from here to there,' and it will move, and nothing will be impossible for you."*

"Well, that bothered me because I had faith, but I could not imagine myself being able to move mountains. It made no sense to me. I remembered what Napoleon Hill said about faith, that it can be induced through repeated suggestions to the subconscious mind. It must be developed. And it was the immortal Emerson who said, "The *whole course of things goes to teach us faith. We need only obey. There is guidance for each of us, and by lowly listening, we shall hear the right word."* Since I trusted these sources, I began a serious attempt to increase my faith by stating over and over that I could indeed move mountains."

"The mountain I most wanted to move wasn't a mountain at all–I wanted to reach millions by sharing my book."

"Another thing was, Lydia Bon told me when we talked, that she intended to go to the police. I told her she was free to do as she pleased. I might have encouraged her. I was determined to stand on my conviction that everything would work out. Before she left, I gave her a large amount of money-not to buy her silence, but to help her live out her life in good fashion."

"When she did go to the police, I was a bit worried, I'll admit. But I held on to my belief that everything would be okay."

"It was amazing that, when everything was seemingly falling apart, I found a light in the darkness. That light was the press clambering for stories about me, and book sales climbing faster than anyone could imagine. Millions of people were reading my book all over the world. What had seemed impossible was now reality, and it was like moving mountains. I was amazed to learn how powerful faith can be."

As he looked out the window at the crowd of reporters gathered near his gate… Little Joe said, "You know, I have had success in my writing career, but never in my wildest dreams could I have imagined myself this well-known. I believed I could move mountains, and the mountains began to move. I wanted to honor my family, and I've done that." Turning to the fireplace, he placed the stained mason jar with the note from his mother in its place of honor on the mantel.

As the fire danced and crackled in the hearth, Little Joe turned again to his family. Picking up a copy of his book and holding it close to his heart, he said, "They lived and loved and made their mark on this world. They're all gone now—the gold is gone—and all that remains are the memories within these pages."

"I missed Mom and Dad, my brothers and sister, so deeply it hurt. From that deep sorrow came a documentation of their lives, and that gives me a kind of peace. Through the study of ancestry, I was able to learn about my great-grandfather and even my great-great-grandfather, Tennessee, and their families. It gave them a more prominent role in my life. It brought us all closer, and now, they, too, give me strength. I produced a treasured personal keepsake because my family was the true '*Family Gold*'. When I remember them, I feel truly rich."

"But are they gone? No, they live right here! If you listen, you can hear them."

Turning his head slightly and lifting the book to his ear, Little Joe grinned and said,

"I can hear them. Tennessee Adams rides again."

Historical Additions to the Third Edition

As *The Family Gold* continues to reach new readers, I'm proud to include several remarkable historical documents in this third edition—each offering deeper insight into the real people and events that inspired the story.

The first is a rare article from The Comet, a newspaper, printed in Johnson City, Tennessee, on October 19, 1899, more than 126 years ago. Written by Magistrate Robert Bailey, it recounts a charming "moonlight marriage" he officiated between his cousin, Nate Adams, and Mary Livingston. This vivid firsthand account—preserved in Bailey's own words—adds authenticity and warmth to the family legacy at the heart of the novel.

The second addition includes a photograph of Tennessee Adams and his wife, Mandy Cox Christie Adams, along with a copy of the original newspaper funeral notice for Tennessee Adams—a pivotal figure in the ancestral line that shaped the story. Though brief, the notice offers a poignant connection to the real life and legacy of a man whose name echoes throughout these pages.

These rare finds were uncovered by my wife and fellow researcher, Victoria Corbin, during our time working in the research department at East Tennessee State University in Johnson City, Tennessee. Her dedication and insight continue to breathe life into the stories behind the novel.

As a special honor, East Tennessee State University purchased the very first copy of The Family Gold for its research department—a gesture that affirms the historical significance woven into the fiction.

Together, these additions serve not only as historical validation but also as a heartfelt tribute to the generations of real people whose lives inspired The Family Gold.

Jerry D. Corbin

Moonlight Marriage.

Wednesday evening about dusk we started out in our magisterial capacity upon a journey fraught with much happiness for at least

> "Two souls with but a single thought,
> Two hearts that beat as one."

We were accompanied by M. Jackson and Uncle Tennessee Adams who acted as pilot. After driving as far as we could through East Carnegie toward sunrise we hitched and footed it across a deep ravine and up a steep hill to the top of a high knob, through a country no one would dare go except to get married or get a divorce and soon stopt at the door of James Adams. All the neighbors had preceded us and the yard was full of people who, while waiting for the bridal party, spent the time in dancing on the ground to a banjo and fiddle accompaniment.

When all was ready for the ceremony the party was drawn up in the form of a horse-shoe radiating from either side of the porch. The bride and groom, Miss Mary Livingston and Mr. Nat Adams, stood on the porch with the attendants, Miss Tiney Able and Mrs. Sam Sneed, on either side. We stood in the center of the circle with M. Jackson in the back-ground and there, in the open air, on top of a knob cut off from sight of civilization by other knobs, with fair Luna shedding her soft beams upon the party and the clock a ticking inside, as if to make Luna-ticks of us all, we pronounced the ceremony that made one of this loving twain. After the ceremony the guests were invited to the dining room where an immense feast had been prepared and was soon devoured. Every good thing was there and everything there was good. Speaking for ourself, M. Jackson and Bob Bailey and wife, we can say the feast was heartily enjoyed, and join the other friends in wishing the newly wedded couple a long life of happiness.

M. Jackson eat so much that he had to complain of an ingrowing toenail in order to get to rest.

Tennessee Adams and his wife, Mandy Cox Christie Adams
Tennessee died August 21st. 1924

TENNESSEE ADAMS DIED THURSDAY

Aged Resident of Johnson City Passed Away at Home of Son Thursday. Funeral in Charge Of Rev. Carroll.

Tennessee Adams passed away at the home of his son, Thomas Adams Thursday afternoon at 4:30 o'clock. He had been ill for several weeks and the end was expected by his relatives.

Mr. Adams was born in the early part of the 18th century and had almost reached the century mark. He confessed religion and joined the Baptist church about 35 years ago and just recently moved his membership to the Unaka Avenue Baptist church. Rev. Carroll of that church will have chrage of the funeral.

His surviving children all live in Johnson City. They are: Mrs. Arthur Sneed, Mrs. Frank Fern, Tom, Jim, Sam and Henry Adams. Two sons and a daughter died some time ago. He is also survived by 34 grand-children, 78 great, grand-children and 4 great, great, grand-children.

Ungrammatical

The Lady—Hobo, did you notice that pile of wood in the yard?

"Yes'm, I seen it."

"You should mind your grammar. You mean you saw it."

"No'm. You saw me see it, but you ain't seen me saw it."—The Christian Evangelist (St. Louis.)

Published in the Johnson City Chronicle August 24, 1924

Bio

Jerry Corbin is the writer, producer, and host of *Building Memories* on WXED 107.3 FM in Ellwood City, Pennsylvania. Streaming live at www.wxedfm.com.

He's currently working on a powerful episodic memoir titled *The Miracle Boy*, where he shares his personal journey of surviving lung cancer — stories of grit, grace, and faith.

When he's not writing or behind the mic, Jerry enjoys shooting pool, loves to travel and sing anytime, anywhere.

Follow his work at www.jerry-corbin.com or linktr.ee/JDCorbin, and email him at **JerryCorbinPM@gmail.com** for updates on upcoming releases.

IMPORTANT NOTICE

If you enjoyed my book, please leave a review on Amazon or your favorite book site. Reviews are incredibly important and deeply appreciated.

www.ingramcontent.com/pod-product-compliance
Lightning Source LLC
Chambersburg PA
CBHW032256310726
48973CB00008B/2428